PROMISES

BOOK FOUR OF
MURPHY'S LAWLESS

Kacey Ezell

Beyond Terra Press
Virginia Beach, VA

Chris Kennedy/Beyond Terra Press
2052 Bierce Dr.
Virginia Beach, VA 23454
http://chriskennedypublishing.com/

Publisher's Note: This is a work of fiction. Names, characters, places, and incidents are a product of the author's imagination. Locales and public names are sometimes used for atmospheric purposes. Any resemblance to actual people, living or dead, or to businesses, companies, events, institutions, or locales is completely coincidental.

Cover Design by J Caleb Design.

Edited by Charles E. Gannon

Ordering Information:
Quantity sales. Special discounts are available on quantity purchases by corporations, associations, and others. For details, contact the "Special Sales Department" at the address above.

Promises/Ezell -- 1st ed.
ISBN: 978-1648550386

Always to EZ, the hero of my story.

Book Four

Promises

By Kacey Ezell

MISSION LOG

UPDATE, MISSION DAY 055
MAJOR R.Y. MURPHY, CO, RECORDING

SUMMARY AO DATA, 55 TAURI B 3 (R'Bak)
LOCAL YEAR: 672 SR (Date coding note: SR stands for "Since Rev."
   Origin of "SR" uncertain. Could refer to spaceside locals' first of-
   ficial recording of years (i.e., revolutions around the local star),
   the political revolts that compelled the SpinDogs to leave R'Bak,
   or the founding of their first rotational habitat, or rohab.)
LOCAL DATE: Day 058 (of 369) (Time sync note: Local days are
   only 18 hours. Consequently, the local year of 369 days is actually only 75 percent the duration of one Earth year.)
EARTH DATE: September 7, 2125 AD

PREOP/STRATEGIC SITREP (approximate):
Increasing competition among powers in the primary system (Jrar)
   may have prompted several nations on the main planet (Kulsis)
   to move up the timetable on exploitation of R'Bak during the
   imminent Searing. First mission arrived in this system (secondary star, Shex) 18 months earlier than on any previous Searing.
   ELINT and SIGINT both indicate that the OpFor is from Kulsis'
   second largest power, which has an entente/détente relationship with the greatest/oldest/traditionalist power.
Due to OpFor's early arrival at R'Bak, SpinDog and RockHounds
   (two different branches of the spaceside local population) had
   neither instituted full cessation of travel nor completed re-
   concealment of stationary assets. Many were compelled to go
   into hiding wherever they were, including various resource col-
   lection teams on the second planet, V'dyr, and one trade mission concluding business on R'Bak.

MISSION DAY UPDATES
000 Ship carrying Lost Soldiers (Dornaani hull *Olsloov*) arrives in
   system, scans, discovers SpinDogs on far side of local sun
   (Shex). Observes, decodes comms. Language is quickly identi-

7

fied as a devolved form of Ktor as it was spoken almost 1,400 years ago (approximation only). Despite linguistic roots, *Olsloov* command staff deems it unlikely that the SpinDogs would become aggressive or that they have had any recent contact with the Ktoran Sphere.

001 Contact made by *Olsloov* command staff. Purpose: acquire consumables.

002 No response, but Spin/Rock ships move to avoid further LoS/lascom messages. Pickets of harvesters/raiders notice movement of the previously undetected Spin/Rock craft, begin maneuvering at extremely high gee (often 2–3, sustained) to effect intercept. Terran cadre analyzes the situation; *Olsloov* selectively jams OpFor broad-comms. Only transmission completed by OpFor was decrypted as "Investigating local anomaly; stand by for details." Narrow-beam comms blocked by position of companion star (Shex), which occluded receivers located in the primary (Jrar) system.

003 Sensor results from *Olsloov* indicate that OpFor's hi-gee maneuvers are consistent with a) intercept of SpinDog craft and b) repositioning to clear transmission coordinates to Jrar. Capt. Mara Lee, USAF, is restored from cryogenic suspension to assist in battlefield support and liaison duty with SpinDog matriarchy.

004 Contact established with Spin/Rock leadership using Dornaani translation system to update language from classic Ktor and to crack cyphers. Agreement reached. Compromised Spin/Rock craft adjust course to flee toward prearranged coordinates in outer system. Intercept trajectory for OpFor intersects optimal ambush point for *Olsloov* and her drones/ROVs. Captain Lee receives partial accelerated training in local language via virtuality immersion.

006 OpFor pursuit elements ambushed by *Olsloov* at edge of outer system. Tech superiority of *Olsloov* and her deployed assets results in complete elimination of enemy hulls without loss or significant damage. In and near R'Bak orbit, Dornaani ROVs (with direct oversight from Captain Lee) assist Spin/Rock assets to eliminate small number of OpFor hulls (mostly interface

transports) and sensors. Dornaani standoff drones eliminate two planetside comm arrays with potential to reach Jrar system.

007 *Olsloov* arrives on-station at R'Bak, conducts close survey for further planetside comm facilities with inter-system capability. None located. AARs generated and shared between *Olsloov* and Spin/Rock cadres.

008 Data sharing and first meetings between *Olsloov* and Spin/Rock leadership. Mutual support and joint operation agreements reached. Captain Lee is debriefed by *Olsloov* cadre and resumes accelerated language training via virtuality technology.

009 Transfer of volatiles and other consumables to *Olsloov* commences. Captain Lee completes accelerated language training.

010 Data packets for tech sharing and replication of 20th century Earth weapons and systems relayed to and declared operational by Spin/Rock automated production facilities. Examples of each system are provided from legacy examples carried aboard *Olsloov*. Legacy examples include helicopters, weapons, ammunition, simple electronics. Captain Lee commences training of first class of SpinDog rotary wing pilots.

013 Major RY Murphy restored from cryogenic suspension. Debrief commences.

014 Major Murphy debrief ends. Light company of Lost Soldiers detached for R'Bak ops is revived.

015 R'Bak ops contingent (Lost Soldiers) commences accelerated language training aboard *Olsloov*. *Olsloov* and seeded (permanent) microsat net detect upswing in movement by advanced vehicles on surface of R'Bak.

016 First planetside training sorties of SpinDog RWP pilots led by Captain Lee. Planetside movement increase is confirmed as OpFor activity. Spin/Rock intel assessment is that they are gathering resources to secure optimum construction site for transmitter capable of reaching Jrar system.

017 Guildmother/Matriarch of leading Spin/Rock Family reported to *Olsloov* as MIA planetside on R'Bak while conducting undisclosed SAR ops in north polar extents. Capt. Lee is cleared for, and tasked to, effect recovery of Guildmother/Matriarch, attached personnel, and others requiring rescue.

018 Capt. Lee's recovery mission achieves objective while sustaining moderate casualties, but Guildmother/Matriarch had been mortally wounded prior to her arrival in AO.

019 *Olsloov* cadre, Lost Soldier CO Murphy, and SpinDog leadership agrees to conops of joint contact and recruitment mission to R'Bak. Objective: gather sufficient indigenous forces and commandeer cached Kulsis equipment to disrupt and prevent OpFor construction of dirtside inter-system comm array. Spaceside requirements articulated; assets identified. Preps begin. Construction of improvised meteoritic assault capsules commences, with limited assistance from Dornaani and contemporary Terrans. Mission leadership selected and briefed. Training commences.

021 Lost Soldier R'Bak detachment completes language training, skills assessment, physical readiness conditioning, and is officially stood up as an active unit. Designation pending.

022 *Olsloov* completes replenishment activities, prepares for departure. Training for joint mission to R'Bak concludes. Objectives and targets updated. Final briefing.

023 *Olsloov* departs.

024 Mission dropship commences op with tug boost toward R'Bak along retrograde orbital track.

028 Orbital insertion successful. Joint mission under command of Lt. Harold Tapper confirmed as maneuvering to establish contacts with Sarmatchani nomads.

036 SpinDog transport shuttles conduct high angle insertion to R'Bak north polar regions, followed by subsonic overland NOE flight to convey task force under Cpt. Hubert Moorefield to border of Hamain desert region in northern hemisphere. Cpt. Moorefield establishes and assumes command of Camp Stark FOB, proximal to anticipated rendezvous point with Lt. H. Tapper.

045 Lt. H. Tapper coordinates and conducts successful Sarmatchani strike against elements of J'Stull satrapy. Mission-critical Kulsian vehicle cache, along with relevant operational supplies, taken and being convoyed to elements from Camp Stark.

046 Seized vehicles and supplies are transferred to Cpt. Moorefield, CO Camp Stark, at rendezvous point. J'Stull pursuit/attack repulsed after suffering heavy losses. Abandoned and reclaimable equipment includes APCs, light ACVs, and company-level personal gear, including Kulsian small arms. Note: otherwise unbreakable draught creatures (*whinaalani*) allow themselves to be ridden by our personnel. Casualties: 11 WIA, 1 WIA/ND ("non-deployable"), 4 KIA.

055 Counter-intelligence operation carried out by Chalmers and Jackson interdicted J'Stull attempt at covert interception of strike assets en route to main objective from Camp Stark. (See Tab #1 in classified addenda.)

* * * * *

Prologue

*R*eminders of home are a double-edged sword.

For some reason, that thought popped into Mara's head, fully formed and apropos of nothing as the song on her Walkman flipped from her usual hard-driving classic rock to a poppy, groovy number by Deee-Lite. Her son had loved the song, though he'd innocently missed all the innuendos involved in the lyrics. That's how it worked when you were only four.

"Captain Mara Lee?"

Grateful for the distraction, Mara hit the pause button on the Walkman and pulled the headphones off. She levered herself up on her bunk and looked toward the figure silhouetted in the doorway.

"Yeah?"

"Major Murphy's compliments, and he wishes to speak with you."

A chorus of *oohs* arose from the other women in the bunk bay, and Mara snorted and grinned, despite the melancholy direction her thoughts had started to take. She got to her feet and lifted both middle fingers in response, laughing along with the others as they rolled over and went back to whatever they'd been doing. Mara shoved her feet into her boots and tied them quickly before walking toward the hatch, twisting her hair up into a bun as she went.

"Any idea what he wants?" she asked.

"No, ma'am," the young man said, his accent crisp and British. He wore a khaki uniform and the insignia of a WWII-era commando. He was stiff, and seemed not entirely comfortable looking directly at her. Mara glanced down at her own attire and realized her sand-colored flight suit was unzipped nearly to her waist. She let out a tiny sigh and zipped it to the level of her nametag.

She'd been relaxing! Why did it suddenly feel like she'd done something wrong? A discontented mulishness trickled into her mind, and she fought to keep her facial expression pleasant, though, realistically, the best she could probably hope for was "neutral." She'd always had a wicked case of "Resting Bitch Face." Murphy never seemed to care, at least. She supposed that was a silver lining of sorts.

Mara followed the young Tommy to the section of the station Murphy had claimed for his headquarters.

Tommy rapped his knuckles on the door frame as the hatch slid open. He slipped inside. Mara heard the murmur of voices, but since she was standing back from the opening, she couldn't make out distinct words, other than Tommy's clipped, "Yes, sir."

The young soldier stepped back out and turned to her. "You're to go right in, ma'am." He said it in that strange Brit way that made it sound like "mum."

"Thank you," she replied, resisting the urge to be sarcastic or otherwise snarky. Tommy couldn't help what decade he'd been born in any more than she could. She flashed him a smile he probably didn't see—given that he was still avoiding eye contact—and slid past him into the boss' office.

"You wanted to see me, sir?" she asked.

"Bruce. Yes. Please come in. Have a seat." Murphy gestured to the cluster of chairs and a small table that dominated one corner of the room. "Can I get you anything?"

"No, sir," she said. "Thank you." His use of her callsign indicated this wasn't the most formal of meetings, but Mara still had no clue why he'd called her in. So, she sat, but lightly, balancing on the edge of her chair.

"How is the mission prep coming, Captain?"

Mara let out a breath and dutifully took him through the primary and contingency plans she and her fellow crews had worked up over the past few weeks. She was careful, thorough, and detailed, and damn sure she didn't miss anything as she filled him in.

Murphy nodded thoughtfully, his eyes on the tabletop. Then he raised them so they were boring straight into her own.

"That sounds very promising. But it all hinges on one detail you've assumed in your report. Namely, that all the SpinDogs will show up to play their part." He leaned back in his chair, his eyes unblinking as he waited for her response.

"They'll be there, sir." Mara fought not to fidget under his intense regard, looking directly into her commander's eyes. "I can promise you that." She could, too. She knew it as sure as she knew her own name.

"Promise. The biggest two-syllable word in the English language." He still did not blink. "Strange word, too. Such a straightforward definition in the dictionary, and yet it always seems to have caveats and limitations connected to it. Like the promises made when people get married. Sometimes all the vows and oaths are kept, and no one gets surprised or hurt. But sometimes the words mean different things to different people, and they don't realize it. Some people make promises knowing they'll break them, or they already have—and there's always the escape clause. Because it's kind of hard to know just what 'until death do us part' means when, just a few months later, a couple can sign some papers and get a divorce."

Finally, he smiled. "So, tell me, Bruce, how's our marriage to the SpinDogs? Specifically, how's that final oath? 'Til death do us part?'"

Mara saw the smile, saw the way it didn't quite reach all the way to his eyes. She took a deep breath and straightened her spine.

"Sir," she said slowly, careful to shade her tone with respect, "you made me their liaison. You're asking me if we have a good relationship with them? Is that right? If they'll fight beside us? I'm telling you they will, but from the way you're asking the question, it sounds like you don't quite believe me. Or maybe you want proof? Is that it?"

His smile became slightly brittle. "I don't have a degree in theology, but I'm pretty sure that since a promise is a matter of free will, not even God could prove whether or not a person is going to keep it." He leaned forward. "And, as impressed as I am with your abilities, Bruce, I don't think walking on water is likely to be one of them.

"However, you clearly believe that you *know* what the SpinDogs mean when they promise to be by our side in the coming shitstorm. So much so that you are clearly willing to risk your life on that understanding and their oath keeping. Even though you've only known them for a month or two."

The remaining fragments of his smile disappeared. "I've watched you, Bruce. You don't trust easily. Which I consider to be a good thing, particularly in this situation. And yet, you trust the SpinDogs more than you trust the majority of us. So no, I'm not asking for proof that they're going to do what they say; I'm asking why you are so certain they will."

He leaned back again. His expression was disturbingly neutral. "Maybe it's time to tell me what really happened at the end of that training assignment. The whole truth, and nothing but the truth...so help you God."

Mara froze and willed her face to stay blank, her eyes to be unwavering while her thoughts whirled and spilled over each other in a chaotic jumble. After an interminable moment, she inhaled slowly through her nose and forced herself to speak.

"All right," she said. "You're right, sir. There is more to the story than what's in my report. But it's not military details. It's...personal."

He didn't move. He just waited with that penetrating gaze for her to begin.

* * * * *

Chapter One

Two Months Earlier

"You sure about this, ma'am?"

Mara didn't turn her head to look in Elroy's direction as he spoke. Instead, she continued standing with her arms crossed over her chest, watching as the SpinDog shuttle made its final approach to the center of their brand spanking-new training camp. She did, however, unbend enough to tilt her head a tiny bit toward him, so he could hear her over the sound of the shuttle's engines. "El, have you been sure of *anything* since we woke up?"

Elroy snorted behind her, acknowledging her point.

"Exactly," she said. "But Murphy's sure about one thing—and he's right. We can't go at this alone. And so far, the SpinDogs seem to be our best option for allies. If that means teaching them to fly helicopters, then I'm gonna teach them to fly helicopters. They can't be any worse than some of the FID students I've dealt with."

"FID?" Elroy asked.

"Foreign Internal Defense. Um...I think you guys called them MAAG in Vietnam."

"Oh, yeah. Those guys. You did that crazy shit?"

"Little bit," Mara said, noncommittal out of habit. "A few years ago. It's why I know how to fly the N-model Huey."

"Nice. I always knew you were a bad mamma jamma, ma'am," Elroy said, and it was Mara's turn to let out a short laugh.

"Always, El?" she asked. They'd known each other less than a week.

"Always since I saw you fly."

"That might be the nicest thing you've ever said to me, El," Mara said. "Now let's smile pretty for our guests."

"Yes, ma'am."

Mara schooled her face into the half-pleasant, half-intimidating expression she'd perfected for meeting new students. She knew that Elroy stood a half-step behind her, in a near-identical pose, with his own menacing scowl firmly in place. Six-foot-five inches and 290 pounds of ebony-skinned muscle, Sergeant Elroy Frazier towered over her, but his placement and posture said clearly that he was on *her* side and subordinate to her in rank.

Little subtleties like that mattered in Mara's experience. Especially during a first impression.

After angling under the camo-netting that mimicked the vegetative cover common at R'Bak's poles, the SpinDog craft set down with enviable lightness and cut its engines. As the noise abated, a hatch opened in the side and a single figure emerged and walked toward them. As soon as she could discern details, Mara found herself blinking in surprise.

"Is that one of our guys?" she asked, voice pitched low. "He looks too big to be a SpinDog!"

"He ain't that big," Elroy said, and Mara had to fight a smile.

Maybe he didn't match up to Elroy's gargantuan frame, but the man walking up to them was quite a bit larger than any of the other space-dwelling men Mara had yet encountered. He had to top six feet, easy, and he was far too powerfully built to have grown up in the .75-gee of their long, rolling asteroid habitats. But he wasn't one of theirs—wasn't a Lost Soldier—and he wore the utilitarian coveralls sported by SpinDog shuttle pilots.

He strode confidently up to Mara and Elroy and came to a rigid position of attention about a meter in front of them. Then he brought his right hand up in the salute that both of the ex-US service members recognized and waited.

"Sir, Pilot Ozendi reports as ordered."

He spoke the English words with a harsh, clipped accent. Softened from the sound of the old Ktoran Mara had learned in the Dornaani's virtual language sims, but its origins were clear. More importantly, she understood the salute for what it was. She snapped to her own position of attention and returned it.

"Please, stand at ease," she said in bastardized Ktoran. Ozendi dropped his hand, and his face split in a wide grin that flashed white against his bronze complexion.

"I learned English from one of your soldiers named Vat," he said, speaking in his own language. "But your, er, 'classic' Ktoran is very good."

"Thank you," Mara said. "I know Vat; he's a friend of mine. We've been waiting for you. Are you alone?"

"Yes," he said. "I will learn your machine and then I will teach others. It was decided."

"That's not what we were briefed," Mara said. "We were expecting a full class."

"The class will come after I learn."

"I see," Mara said. She drew in a deep breath and took a moment to study the man in front of her. With his size, the color of his skin, and his wide, easy grin, something about him tugged at her memory. Her ex's bronzed, beautiful male face coalesced in her mind's eye, laughing at something she said as he shook seawater out of his eyes. Unexpected pain flared bright and hot in her gut.

"I don't suppose you surf, do you?" she asked, without really meaning to do so.

"I do not know what that is."

"Never mind." She shook her head slightly to clear it. "It's nice to meet you, Ozendi. I'm Captain Mara Lee. This is my crew chief, Sergeant Frazier. And this," she said, turning slightly, "is the mighty Bell UH-1 Iroquois. You can call her 'Huey.'"

Ozendi tilted his head to the side and looked from Mara to the helicopter and back again. "Why do you use the word 'her?' It is a machine, is it not?"

Mara smiled thinly. "Yes," she said. "*She* is a machine. But ask any Huey pilot, and they'll tell you that *she* has a soul. You'll learn, and until you do, I'd appreciate it if you'd use the proper terms out of respect. This old warrior, and others like her, have saved a lot of lives over the years."

"Including mine," Elroy rumbled behind her.

Ozendi's eyebrows pinched together in a frown. "But this is not proper. A machine does not have intelligence or a personality. You cannot speak of it as if it does."

Mara's smile grew. "Tell you what, hotshot," she said, "when you're teaching me how to fly your aircraft, you can call it whatever you like. But if you want to fly my bird, you'll do as I say. Sergeant Frazier will get you settled into your quarters and issue you the gear you need. Be back here in an hour to start academics."

She didn't wait for a reply, simply turned on her heel and walked back toward the low-slung building that functioned as the headquarters of the tiny operation. She had to call Murphy and inform him that the SpinDogs had changed the plan. And she needed a moment to collect herself and get her shit together.

Why did the damn student have to look so much like her ex-husband?

* * *

After about a week of academics, Mara realized that Ozendi didn't look all that much like Cam after all, other than the fact that they were both built like Polynesian warrior gods. Cam had always been light-hearted and easygoing, which had balanced nicely with Mara's driven intensity in the early years of their marriage. Ozendi, on the other hand, was every bit as focused as she and had a healthy dose of the competitive nature she'd glimpsed among their SpinDog allies. Especially when dealing with Elroy, which Mara found to be equal parts amusing and annoying. But it was a personality quirk, and like all personality quirks, it presented an opportunity for exploitation if she paid attention.

And Mara had learned to always pay attention. Which was why she and Ozendi were walking out to the bird alone today, despite Elroy's vociferous protestations.

"Ma'am," he'd said, using his hardest-edged tone. "Major Murphy charged me with your safety. You can't be serious."

"I'm absolutely serious, El," she'd replied, slamming her locker closed for emphasis. She leaned down to stuff her helmet in its bag and straightened back up, her eyes hard. "You're not going. End of story."

"But how can I—"

"Keep me safe? That's a damn good question. Do you have a set of controls in the back, Sergeant Frazier?" she'd asked, raising her eyebrows, and letting her tone dip down into the glacial range.

"No, but—"

"But what? What the fuck do you think you're going to do back there, then, hm? Learning to hover is arguably the most dangerous thing the student pilot will do. Putting you on the bird exposes you to unnecessary risk without any corresponding reward. Whereas I, as a competent and trained instructor pilot seated at a set of controls, have the ability to prevent the student from crashing the aircraft and injuring or killing us both. However, that job will be infinitely easier if he's not also trying to show off for you because of whatever stupid man-competition thing you guys have going on between you. So you, Sergeant, will *sit your ass down and wait for me to land*. Is that clear?"

Mara had watched as a muscle in El's cheek jumped in his otherwise impassive face. But he'd nodded and left without giving her any more grief. She'd have to smooth his ruffled feathers later, she knew. Right now, though, she had other things on her mind.

"So," she said as she and her student approached the nose of the helicopter, "are you ready for this?"

"Absolutely," Ozendi replied, flashing her that confident grin of his. "I look forward to it."

"Remember what I told you," she said. "Soft hands, soft feet."

"Of course, of course," he nodded, but she was pretty sure he wasn't really paying attention. So, she just shrugged and walked around to the left side of the aircraft, opened the door, and plunked her helmet on the seat.

She got her seat set up the way she liked, activated her EFB, scrolled down to the proper checklist page, and then walked back around the bird to join Ozendi. Though she'd been skeptical at first, she had to admit that the concept of having all of her publications on a computer no larger than a pad of paper was a *damn* nice improvement over the paper checklists and pubs she'd always lugged around before, even if it *did* make her feel a little bit like a character on *Star Trek.*

"Right," she said. "Let's preflight her."

Ozendi glanced at Mara's hands where she held her EFB. His face went blank, losing all of the cheerful excitement of the moment before.

"Why do you bring that?" he asked, pointing. "The tablet computer?"

"It's my EFB," she said, startled. He just looked at her, waiting. "Electronic Flight Bag. It's got my checklists and stuff on it. You've seen me use this before. I had it during academics."

"It is merely archival?"

"Y-yes," she said, eyes narrowing. Where was he going with this line of questioning? "But you should know that. Sergeant Frazier gave you one on the first day, when he issued you your helmet!"

"I did not activate it," Ozendi said.

Mara blinked. "Wait—what? You didn't even turn it on?"

"No. I do not trust it."

"But…you went through a whole week of academics! You had to have opened it to study. How else could you possibly have learned your systems knowledge well enough to pass the test?"

"You and Sergeant Frazier taught me. I remembered."

Mara blinked again, her mind reeling. "You mean to tell me that you memorized *everything* we said to you in academics?"

"Yes. So I do not need a computer to tell me what to do."

"The EFB doesn't—" Mara shook her head in frustration and abruptly remembered part of Murphy's initial briefing about this mission. The SpinDogs, he'd said, were *incredibly* leery of automation or AI-assistance. Obsessively so. For that reason, all radio-navigation mods had been removed from the aircraft. Hell, even their comms had been stripped down to very basic, line of sight radios.

"Okay, look," she said, taking a deep breath. She angled the tablet to let Ozendi see the Before Exterior Inspection Checklist on its screen. "This is just archival, like you said. It's not an augmentation or assist of any kind. It's literally just a book displayed on the screen. But this book is important, Ozendi. You can't fly without it, even if you memorize every word I ever say. There's stuff in here that I've never encountered, thank everything that's good. But if I ever *did* encounter it, my best shot at dealing with it is contained here."

Ozendi nodded slowly, but instead of relief or acquiescence, his face assumed a pained look.

"Cannot we just take the book?"

"You mean a physical copy? I don't—we don't have one printed out, and to print it will take…hell, I don't know…several days? But…" she pressed her lips together and made a decision. Murphy may not like it, but he'd been the one to talk about strategic victories when dealing with their new allies, after all.

"Look," she said. "It's important to me that we don't do anything you're uncomfortable with. If you don't want to fly with my EFB, that's fine. We can postpone the flight until we can get you some physical copies of the publications you need. And I *will* get you those. But if you want to go today, maybe you can just trust me that the EFB is just an archival device, like you said?"

Ozendi stared at her, his eyes dark with conflicting emotions. She could tell he wanted to go. He was a pilot, after all. At a certain point, the yearning to fly saturates the self and makes every delay painful.

She smiled and reached out with her free hand to pat his shoulder. "It is up to you, my friend," she said, using that language for the first time in their acquaintance. He started a little at her touch. "I will not push. I want nothing but trust between us if we're going to fly together."

"I trust you," he said, looking as if he spoke without realizing it. "I want to go."

"All right," she said. "Then let's go! And I promise, on my honor, I'll get your paper pubs started as soon as we land."

His smile grew slowly this time, rather than the flashing, cocky grin she'd seen before. This one seemed like something else, something much more genuine.

"Thank you."

"Of course. Now, let's start up top…"

* * *

"Okay, so the first thing we're going to do," Mara said over the Huey's intercom as she smoothly hover-taxied the bird out into a clear field behind the shuttle landing area, "is try out the controls one by one."

"I can take them both," Ozendi said, keying his intercom microphone with his foot after a minute's searching for the switch.

"Well, first of all, there are *three* sets of controls, not two," Mara said as she decreased collective and set them down lightly in the center of the field. "So that's something you need to understand right away. Hovering a helicopter isn't like flying a fixed-wing aircraft. You're keeping the bird in a state of dynamic stability. Here, I'll show you."

She looked over at Ozendi, occupying the seat to her right. He sat up tall, his spine straight, his legs rigid with tension, his feet flat on the heel plates in front of him.

"Look at me," she said. "Turn your head and look. First of all, notice my posture. See how I'm kinda slumped down like this?" She exaggerated the curve of her spine for effect. "Slide your butt forward just a bit on the seat and let yourself bend. She's not the most ergonomically designed aircraft ever, but she gets the job done."

"Like this?" he asked, echoing her posture. Mara grinned and nodded.

"Perfect," she said. "Now, stretch your legs out a little and put the balls of your feet on the crossbars of the pedals—go ahead, you can look. Down there where it says 'Bell' and 'Huey.' And put your heels down on the heel plates. Yes. Good. Now when I tell you to make a pedal movement, I just want you to move your foot—not your whole leg! Just the foot, pivot at your ankle. And if I tell you to 'curl your toes,' I mean just that. Scrunch your toes up in your boot. Understand?"

"Yes, but why—"

"Because, Ozendi, the Huey is a lovely old warbird, but she must be treated like a lady. You have to make very small, very fine muscle movements in order to not overcontrol the aircraft and begin working at cross purposes to yourself. You'll see what I mean here in a minute. Just trust me for now."

She glanced at his face, or what she could see of it beneath his helmet's smoked visor. His lips were twisted in a wry half smile, but he nodded. Good enough.

"Okay, hands. Put your right hand on the cyclic. Again, look over at me. See how my right forearm is anchored on my thigh like this? That's part of the reason for sitting the way we do. You keep your arm locked down like this, and that helps you to make very small, fine movements with your hands. And don't grip the cyclic that tight! I can see your knuckles turning white from here. Hold it like it's an egg, don't strangle it—better. Now look at my hand again. See how I'm waving my bottom three fingers at you? I'm only holding the cyclic with my thumb and forefinger, so that I can key the trigger mic and talk. See? When I tell you to 'wiggle your fingers,' that's what I want you to do, got it?"

Ozendi obediently waggled the middle, ring, and pinky fingers of his right hand at her.

"Perfect, again. Okay, lastly, the collective. This is your vertical movement, got it? You pull up, we go up. You push down, we go down. It's very simple, but it often feels counterintuitive to people used to flying fixed-wing craft. So just remember, up and down are in your left hand. Lateral movement is in your right, and you control where your nose points with your feet."

"I learned these things in academics," Ozendi said, a thread of impatience working through his tone.

"Correction. You *heard* these things in academics. You're about to learn them now. So just follow along on the controls as I pick us up…"

Mara began to smoothly pull up on the collective as she spoke, feeding in a tiny amount of left pedal as she did so. In truth, she didn't even think about the pedals or the collective anymore. The Huey was the first helicopter she'd ever flown, and, at this point, hovering was merely an extension of her thoughts: Mara thought "up" and her body and the machine worked together to pull them up into a stable hover, with her skids hanging exactly four feet above the ground.

"Now what I want you to do," she said, hearing the dreamlike quality in her voice that meant she was speaking while hovering, "is to slowly take control of the cyclic. Your hand is already in place. I just want you to keep us in a stable hover. When you're ready: 'Pilot has the cyclic.'"

"Pilot has the cyclic," Ozendi said, squeezing the trigger mic to speak. That squeezing was enough to cause the hover to wobble backwards, which Ozendi instinctively tried to correct by pushing forward.

"Less forward cyclic." Mara's command was still dreamy; she concentrated on keeping her hand close enough to prevent Ozendi from getting truly out of control. As she'd known he would, he overcorrected and pulled back rapidly on the cyclic. The Huey responded by tilting her nose sharply up and accelerating backward.

"Instructor has the controls," Mara said, grabbing the cyclic and centering it back up in order to gentle the helicopter's movement. The Huey settled, once again, into a stable hover.

"I barely touched it!" Ozendi said, indignant.

"Yep," Mara replied, smiling slightly. "You barely touched her, and yet it was still too much. Remember what I said about not strangling the cyclic? Hold her gently, like a lady."

"Not all ladies like to be touched so softly," he grumbled.

Mara grinned. "Perhaps not," she said. "But this one does. Gentle, Ozendi. You're doing great."

"Am I?" he asked, but he gamely rested just his fingertips on the cyclic again. This time, when Mara gave him the control, he did much better at keeping the Huey centered and stable.

"Good," she said, feeling a smile as she spoke. Teaching a student, *feeling* them getting it…that was the essence of flight instruction. It never got old. "Okay, now, when I tell you, I want you to move us to the right. I'll tell you 'right ten' and I want you to gently feed in right cyclic. We'll start to accelerate in that direction. I'll count down from ten, and when I get to one, you'll have to stop us. Do you understand?"

"I think so."

"Good." Mara twisted in her seat, craning her neck to look over her shoulder through the pinned-open cabin doors of the Huey. "Clear right ten."

With her fingertips on the cyclic, Mara felt him pull the tiniest bit to the right. As was natural, he pulled slightly aft, too, but she used her hand as a barrier to keep him from going too far. She would address that on the next try. For now, she just wanted him to feel how much input he needed to get them going in the right direction. Her feet on the pedals kept the nose pointed steadily ahead as they began to slide across the ground in a sideways hover to the right.

"Five," she called. "Four. Three—start taking your input out—Two. One. Stop right."

It wasn't particularly smooth, and he immediately started to oscillate fore and aft, but Ozendi managed to bring them to a credible stop at the end of her countdown.

"Instructor's controls," Mara said, taking a firmer hold of the cyclic.

"Instructor's controls," Ozendi agreed, letting go.

"IP has the controls," Mara confirmed, and decreased the collective to gently set them down on the grass. "Ozendi!" she said then, letting a bit of the joy she felt into her voice. "That was awesome!"

"It was?" he asked, sounding faintly exhausted. She couldn't help but laugh.

"It damn sure was! Almost no one is able to do that so well their first time. That was fantastic. I'm really proud of you. Now. Ready to add in the collective?"

* * *

By the end of the first day, Ozendi could hover. Oh, it wasn't one hundred percent stable, but he could pick up and set down where he wanted, and he could move laterally and vertically according to the commands Mara gave him. He was a little shaky on controlling the nose with the pedals, but that wasn't unusual for a brand-new student, and Mara was confident he'd improve rapidly. Especially as he was their only student, and they were planning at least one flight every day.

"As soon as the rotor is still, you can go on inside," Mara told Ozendi as the main rotor coasted to a stop during the shutdown sequence. "Sergeant Frazier will help me put the bird to bed, and then we'll join you for a debrief."

"Debrief?" Ozendi asked.

"Yes. It's essential for your learning. We're going to talk about your flight and all of the things you learned in order to reinforce those lessons," Mara said. She couldn't help but give him a sympathetic smile. "Don't worry," she said. "What's said in debrief isn't personal. It's all about making you a better pilot. And we all had to learn at some point."

"And Sergeant Frazier will come?" Ozendi asked, his voice pitched low, as the man himself approached with the long rope used to tie the main rotor down.

"He will," Mara said, her tone hardening. "His expertise is also necessary for your learning."

Ozendi drew in a deep breath but gave her a short nod and said nothing else. Instead, he released his four-point harness and reached for his door handle.

"Ozendi," Mara said, surprising herself. "It was a good flight."

He hadn't yet removed his helmet, so she still couldn't see his entire face, but his lips curved in that genuine smile again, and something warm uncurled deep in her belly at the sight of it.

"Thank you, Mara," he said. "You are a good teacher."

He opened the door and stepped out of the aircraft. He nodded to Sergeant Frazier as the crew chief caught the rotor blade and pulled it down to hook the tie-down rope to the right place. Mara could see Sergeant Frazier's blank, professional face as he returned the nod. Then, as he walked the blade around to where he'd secure it to the tail, his eyes met Mara's, with a question shining clear: *What the hell was that about?*

Mara shrugged and looked down at the aircraft forms in her lap. Honestly, she didn't know, and she wasn't sure she wanted to find out. Fortunately, she had the perfect distraction available as she turned her mind to the mental math required to calculate the time they'd spent flying and hovering. She put her head down and focused on filling out the forms.

It was no use. By the time she finished up the forms, Elroy had tied down the blades, done the appropriate checks, and was standing next to her cockpit door with arms crossed over his chest.

"Well?" he asked when she looked up.

"It was a good flight," she said.

"It musta been. He was beaming like you'd just asked him to the prom."

"He's a pilot, El. He likes to fly. And he did well for his first helicopter lesson. That was him hovering back in here."

"Hmmph, no wonder the nose was hunting all over like a dog trying to catch a scent."

Quick, hot anger rose up inside her, tangling with the normal post-flight fatigue.

"Damnit, El! This is why I didn't bring you along," she said as she swung her legs over the collective and hopped down to the ground outside the bird. Elroy towered over her, but she put her fists on her hips and glared up at him. "I don't know what Ozendi did to piss in your Wheaties, but you need to get over it. Now. He's our student, and this is an important step toward building the strategic partnership that Murphy—and others—think we need to survive. I don't care what you have to do, but get your shit together, all right? I don't have time for this crap!"

Elroy met her glower for glower, but Mara held her ground. She'd never been one to be intimidated into backing down, especially not when she knew she was right.

Finally, eventually, Elroy wilted just a bit.

"You're right, ma'am," he said softly. "And I'm sorry. It's just…something about that guy rubs me the wrong way."

"Can you put your finger on what?" Mara asked, allowing her tone to soften slightly. "Instincts are important, and I'm inclined to trust yours, but you've got to meet me halfway, here, El."

"It's just…he don't look at you right." Elroy shuffled his feet slightly. "I mean, I don't think he'd ever try anything…but I watch him watch you, and he ain't looking at you like one pilot looks at another. He looks at you like a man looks at a pretty woman."

Mara's eyebrows went up. "Are you telling me Ozendi's checking out my rack?" she asked dryly.

"No, ma'am. He's checking out your ass."

Mara stifled a laugh and a surge of pure alpha female pride. "Well," she said slowly, "can you blame him? I mean, my ass is pretty spectacular."

Now it was Elroy's turn to look shocked. His mouth dropped open slightly, and for the first time in their acquaintance, he appeared speechless. Mara snorted and let the laugh bubble up from inside her and spill out.

"Hell, Elroy, you should see your face! I'm sorry, man, I didn't mean to short-circuit your brain, but damn, I got you good!"

"Ma'am?" Elroy said slowly. "I don't understand…do you want him to be looking—"

"At my ass? Not particularly, no," Mara said, shaking her head and continuing to chuckle. "But it's not the first time, and I'm sure it won't be the last. Unless you think he's gonna do something inappropriate, I think I can forgive him for sizing me up. As long as he performs to standard, right? Because that's the mission, and that's what matters."

Elroy shook his head slightly, his expression faintly disapproving. "It just don't seem right."

Mara took pity on him and reached out to lay a comforting hand on his big shoulder. "Look, El. The Air Force I served in and the Army you served in were very different entities. But men and women don't change. Like I said, he can look all he wants, as long as he's respectful and performs to the standard. The minute he fails to do either of those things, we're on him, right? But people are people, and people are gonna look. Hell, how many times do you think the girls and I checked out your arms and back just after we were all defrosted?"

"You—you did?"

"Mmm hmm. You were Irina's favorite of the MACV-SOG guys. She called you 'Hot Chocolate.'"

He snorted softly, rolling his eyes, but his lips quirked up in a smile.

"So," Mara said, "we good?"

"Yes, ma'am," he said. "We're good. I'll lay off the Spin jock. I'm gonna keep watching him close, though."

"I wouldn't expect any less."

Mara flashed a grin at him, then she turned and grabbed her helmet from the hook above her seat. Elroy fell into step beside her as they headed to the temporary building that had been set up as their operations center. It was just a prefab building, camouflaged with the local shrubs and trees that made up the forest around them. Mara couldn't have said if they were deciduous or coniferous plant forms since they seemed to look like both and neither at the same time. What they were, though, was prolific, which was interesting, given the overall character of the dry, desert planet. Here at the poles, however, the climate was more temperate—a fact for which Mara thanked her lucky stars. She'd done more than enough time in Africa and the Middle East to relish operating in cracked, dusty heat. It was a nice change, having their little training facility tucked in a valley between forested hills and set next to a clear mountain stream; it was pretty, and Mara liked to be in pretty surroundings. Even if they were, according to Murphy, over a hundred-fifty light years from home.

The interior of the building, however, looked much like every deployed tactical operations center she'd ever set foot in: utilitarian beige walls, ugly linoleum flooring, communications wiring stapled along the corner between wall and ceiling or wall and floor. Mara strode all the way down the hallway to the small locker room on the left, where she dumped her gear before hitting the restroom and meeting the two men in the larger room they used for briefings and lessons.

"All right," she said as she walked in. Both Ozendi and Elroy came quickly to their feet in response. She waved a hand to indicate they should sit and took her own chair at the head of the table. "Let's go through this from the beginning."

As they talked, Mara remained mindful of Elroy's warnings about Ozendi's attitude toward her. She took care to keep her own tone brisk and businesslike, but that didn't seem to faze her student at all. He still smiled that wide, warm smile that shone through his dark eyes. When she spoke, he listened intently, even taking notes here and there. He accepted her criticisms and corrections with good grace, even when Elroy chimed in with his perspective as a back-end flyer.

At the end of the debrief, she sat back in her chair and folded her hands in her lap.

"Now," she said, per her usual custom. "It's your turn. How was my instruction? Was there anything that I could have done to make it easier for you to learn today?"

Ozendi looked up from his notebook, where he'd been scribbling down her last few points.

"Better?" he asked, sounding surprised. "No! Not at all. You are a good instructor, Mara. I said this before."

"Thank you," Mara said, studiously avoiding Elroy's eyes. "But even good instructors can improve. Every flight offers the opportunity to learn, right? That's true for me, too. So, tell me, what should I learn from you?"

Ozendi looked at her for a long moment, his smile softening, then fading away as the look in his eyes grew more intense.

"I cannot think of anything right now," he eventually said. "But I will let you know."

"Good enough," Mara said, ignoring the flutter in her stomach. She was just hungry after the flight was all. She pushed her chair back from the table and stood up. Both Elroy and Ozendi followed her lead. "I'll see you back here tomorrow morning then," she said. "El, walk with me."

"Yes, ma'am," Elroy said. He stepped quickly to follow her out the door, leaving Ozendi staring after her.

* * * * *

Chapter Two

Training progressed. Mara taught Ozendi the basics of hovering and forward flight, as well as what to do in a number of emergency situations. The one thing she couldn't really teach was instrument flying. For one thing, R'Bak didn't have a network of radio-navigation stations…or really any at all. The SpinDogs were so skittish about stray radio signatures that there was no way for her to build even the most basic of instrument approaches or routes. For the time being, at least, it appeared that they were limited to VFR operations and navigation only.

She largely concentrated on what had been called "mission skills" when she'd learned to fly the Huey. This mostly consisted of VFR navigation at both high and low altitudes, as well as operations in unprepared landing areas under various terrain and threat scenarios. They started with the basics and eventually worked up to flying long, circuitous routes in and around the hilly, forested regions near the pole.

They were still limited, however, by their fuel capacity.

"Mara," Ozendi said to her one day, when they were planning a training route for the next day. "I want to go here." He stabbed his finger down on the terrain map, indicating a valley higher up in the mountains to their west.

"We don't have the legs for that, Ozendi," Mara said. "You know that. We go out that far, we won't get back to the camp here before we flame out from fuel starvation."

"What if we refuel at this location, then? We can fly in these mountains and identify some very good high elevation LZs. Excellent training!" He flashed his grin at her, the one he used when he was trying to be charming and persuasive. Mara smiled back, even though the grin didn't have the same effect on her insides as his softer, more genuine smile.

Not that *that* thought was helpful. Mara forced her focus back to what Ozendi was saying.

"It would be, but I doubt there is a cache of JP-8 in that random mountain valley, Ozendi."

"No, but there could be, if we put some there."

"What are you talking about?"

"This location is known to my people," he said. "It is one of our contacts. I can have fuel positioned there for our use. It is part of the overall plan to establish flying bases throughout this region, yes? My people already cache vehicles there. It makes sense to have helicopters as well."

Mara looked down at the map, considering. He was right about the location. It *would* make an excellent air ops base for mountain training, and its distance from their current location meant that if they *did* have refueling capability there, it would effectively double their range.

"It's a good idea," she said slowly. "But I have to speak to my leadership about it before we do anything."

"Of course," Ozendi said, his smile triumphant. "You must call Major Murphy at once."

She laughed. "Not so fast, hot shot. We're following *your* people's comm security schedule. My next contact is tomorrow afternoon. That's soon enough. In the meantime, go ahead and plan the training sortie. Make sure you pick at least three possible LZs with various characteristics. Make one a pinnacle if you can. We'll see if we can actually get into any of them. We'll talk about terrain masking and threat mitigation along the route, too."

"And what will you do?" he asked.

Mara stopped short, drew herself up and let her face and voice go icy. "Why?"

"Because…" he hesitated, spread his hands and gave a little laugh. "Because I like working beside you more than working without you."

She let her eyebrows go up.

"Well," she said. "That's very flattering, but I have things to do, and you're perfectly capable of coming up with a decent plan."

"Are you sure you wouldn't rather just oversee my efforts? Just in case?"

"In case of what?" she asked. "You know how to do this, Ozendi. You don't need me to hold your hand."

"Perhaps not," he said with a ghost of his cocky grin. "But perhaps I would enjoy you holding my hand."

She snorted softly. "Are you flirting with me?"

"Yes," he said, and he blinked his eyes slowly as his smile grew. Not for the first time, she noticed the sweep of his very long, quite beautiful lashes.

It took her a moment to tear her eyes away, but when she did, she rolled them skyward in an exaggerated expression of exasperation.

"Just make a plan, Ozendi. I'll be back later to check on you." She turned toward the door.

"I shall await your return with great eagerness," he called after her.

She ignored him and headed out into the hallway, shaking her head at his audacity.

But she couldn't stop her lips from curving upward in a smile.

* * *

Murphy approved the plan and had further information for her, besides. It seemed the SpinDog leadership was happy with their progress and was looking to accelerate the program. Mara had gained a lot of respect for Murphy since he'd been awakened, but he increased in her esteem when he explained how he'd leveraged this desire into building a more robust support team for their surface-based operations.

"So yes, Bruce, by tomorrow afternoon, you will have your fuel at the settlement your student indicated," Murphy had said. Though his face remained composed and blank, Mara thought she could detect a gleam of triumph in his eyes, even through the transmission's induced distortion. "In addition, we're sending you a larger maintenance response team and a few other SpinDog support personnel. Medical, for one. She's also fluent in English, so she can help with any translation problems that may arise with your incoming student body."

"Incoming when?" she'd asked.

"Twenty days. You'll have to finish Ozendi's training, have the training syllabus validated, and the logistics worked out by then."

"It will be tight, but I should be able to manage, sir. Especially with the additional assets you're sending my way."

Because, of course, the training support wasn't all that Murphy was sending to meet her in the mountains. Her sleepy, tiny little training base was about to get a lot busier as the majority of the Lawless' rotary-wing assets unveiled their capabilities. What had been simply her, Elroy, and a part-time maintenance team would shortly become a full-blown task force.

All under the guise of training the SpinDogs.

Strategically, it was a brilliant move on Murphy's part, for it allowed them to demonstrate their commitment to these new allies, as well as increase their own lethality and planetside capabilities. And, as Mara and Ozendi continued to develop SpinDog helicopter operations, that increase would apply to *their* capabilities as well. Win, win, win.

If Mara could get Ozendi trained up to the appropriate level quickly enough.

So, the cross-country training that they'd planned had gone from "highly desirable" to "mission critical" in a very short period of time. To that end, Mara dispatched Elroy in one of the local ground vehicles to make his way to the settlement Ozendi swore was there. The SpinDog pilot had given Elroy a flat metal disk he'd taken from around his neck to use as a bona fide when he arrived. Apparently presenting the disk, which was stamped with a design Mara didn't recognize, was the only way to not be executed upon arrival.

The settlement was quite protective of its privacy, it seemed.

Mara pushed down her worry and waved goodbye as Elroy drove away, jouncing and bouncing over the unimproved terrain. The man had been MACV-SOG. He could take care of himself. And anyway, Murphy's maintenance response team and support staff should be there by the time he arrived. It shouldn't be an issue.

As Elroy's vehicle disappeared through the trees, Mara turned to look at Ozendi, who had raised his hand in farewell to Elroy.

"Well," she said. "Looks like it's just you and me."

"How fortunate," he replied with a flash of his grin. Mara snorted softly and rolled her eyes, eliciting a laugh from the man.

"Let's go look at your plan," she said. "Show me what you think we can get accomplished."

Ozendi nodded and gestured for her to precede him back to the operations building. Mara started walking in that direction, but slowed so that she paced beside him, rather than ahead of him.

"So, it seems like you and Sergeant Frazier have mended your fences," she said, her voice softening. This wasn't really her business, and she'd talked to Elroy about it, but she was desperately curious about Ozendi's perspective on the relationship. "Or, at least, the two of you aren't growling and bristling at one another anymore."

"Oh!" Ozendi looked over at her and smiled. "I was wondering what 'fences' you were talking about. Yes, Sergeant Frazier and I have come to an understanding. He is very protective of you."

"Sorry about the fences; it's an expression from home," she said, shrugging. "But yes. We're a crew and good friends as well. Part of his mission here is to be my backup. I'm actually surprised he was willing to leave me, even if only for two days."

"That is part of what we talked about before he left. Part of what you call the 'fence mending.' He explained his obligation to keep you safe and asked me to assume that obligation temporarily during his absence."

Mara's eyebrows shot up.

"Oh?" she asked. "How interesting."

"I was willing," Ozendi said. "Such requests are not unknown among my people. When our missions take us from our home stations, it is common to find a trusted friend to assume responsibility for those in one's care. It is a matter of great honor to be so chosen. I was happy to agree to his request."

"Don't be offended," she said, squaring her shoulders as she prepared to speak bluntly. "But I'm honestly surprised he would ask you, since he's been suspicious of your demeanor toward me from the beginning."

To her surprise, Ozendi threw back his head and laughed.

"Yes," he said. "He mentioned that. I reassured him that in my culture to try to sexually take an unwilling woman was to court death, if not from her retaliation, then from the retribution of the station as a whole." He glanced over at her and gave a little shrug. "We are a tightly bound community, and most of us are related to each other, however distantly. Such behaviors are incompatible with our existence, and the punishment for them is to be ejected from the station."

"You mean exiled planetside?" Mara asked, fascinated by this glimpse into SpinDog culture.

"I mean ejected naked from an airlock," Ozendi said baldly, no trace of a smile on his lips now. "As I said, transgressive behaviors are incompatible with our existence."

"Fair enough," Mara said. "But I'll be honest, I don't think Elroy was worried you'd force yourself on me. I think he's more concerned you'll try to seduce me…and even more concerned I'd let you."

"Ah," Ozendi said. Mara waited, but he didn't elaborate. When she glanced up at his face, that warm, beautiful smile was stretched across his mouth once again.

"'Ah?'" she asked.

"Yes," he said, coming to a stop before their building.

"Do you have any other thoughts on the matter?" Mara asked, exasperation leaking into her tone. "Besides 'ah'?"

"One," he said, that smile growing, shining from his eyes.

"And?" she prompted.

"Simply this: Sergeant Frazier is not the type to be unduly concerned…about anything." With that, he reached out and twined his fingers through Mara's, and lifted her hand to eye level. He pressed her knuckles to his forehead and then to his mouth. He brushed his lips across the back of her fingers, and the warmth of his touch rocketed through her, igniting fires under her skin that burned like the light in his dark eyes.

She opened her lips to speak, but for once in her life, she couldn't think of anything to say. Ozendi lowered his right eyelid in a wink, let go of her hand, and disappeared into the building before she could do anything else.

Mara dragged in a deep breath, trying to force her nerves to settle. *Get yourself together, girl,* she ordered. *You've flown with beautiful men before! Never mind that none of them made you feel like you were about to combust just from a single kiss. It's not a big deal. Handle your business!*

With that demand ringing in her metaphorical ears, Mara squared her shoulders and followed Ozendi into the operations building.

* * *

The next morning, at dawn, Mara felt a fluttering in her belly that had nothing whatsoever to do with Ozendi.

The suns rose bright and clear in a cloudless, golden sky. The air was sweet with a tantalizing hint of the heat to come, but a consistent light breeze promised to keep temperatures within the bearable range. It was, as one of Mara's old flight instructors would have said, a cherry day to fly.

Mara pushed aside memories of other perfect days back home and headed out to the aircraft with an eagerness that vibrated through her entire being. Yesterday, she and Ozendi had gone over every detail of his plan—which had been rather good. In hindsight, that really wasn't much of a surprise: life in space meant you either planned well or died fast. And, she had to admit, he was coming along nicely with his flying skills. Before too long, she'd be willing to certify him as a fully qualified aircraft commander. Then they would see if he had what it took to be a flight instructor—but those were questions and problems for another day. Today, they were going to fly and have some fun.

Their first order of business was to make their way to the settlement Ozendi had indicated on the map. From the beginning of this venture, navigation had been a tricky proposition. Back home, Mara would have used radio navigation aids like VHF omni-directional receivers and TACAN military navigation aids to augment her visual "clock/map/ground" dead reckoning navigation. Not to mention the Global Positioning System, which had been an aviation game-changer in the last decade she'd spent on Earth.

But R'Bak didn't have any of those options available. The Dornaani microsats could certainly have served in the same role as the GPS constellations back home, but the SpinDogs' ingrained caution about casual radio contact made that a no-go.

So, she had to rely on other methods. Like most planets, R'Bak had a magnetosphere complete with north and south poles. The Huey had a magnetic—or whiskey, for "wet"—compass mounted high above the pilot's windscreen. She could use that for basic dead-reckoning, although that was a tricky proposition since they were based in the polar region itself. As one would expect, the closer they got to the pole, the less reliable the whiskey compass headings became. Plus, some of the aircraft systems that used electricity induced further errors in the reading, thanks to the electrical current running through the wires also mounted above the windscreen. Basically, Mara could use the whiskey compass as a rough guideline, but she wouldn't want to rely upon it for precise navigation over long distances.

Fortunately, she had two things that *did* seem to be utterly reliable. The first was the incredibly detailed imagery compiled by the SpinDogs over many decades—centuries?—and recently updated by the Dornaani microsats to create excellent navigation maps. Mara had never seen such high-resolution, high-fidelity images, not even from the most highly classified satellite intel back home. With these maps, she could almost navigate tree-by-tree, and, since the indigenous population of R'Bak seemed to be both pre-industrial and—perhaps more importantly—located elsewhere, Mara had little fear of "pop-up" obstacles like towers or powerlines.

The second reliable factor was Ozendi.

"I was born in the settlement we are going to see," he admitted. They were about thirty minutes into their navigation route, winding through the mountains and forests about one hundred meters above the trees. "It is why I was sent to be your first student. I grew up adapted to standard gravity, and it was thought that this would be helpful in learning to fly the atmospheric craft."

"Shit," Mara said as her mind spun from this revelation. "Yeah, it would be. I didn't even think about that, but in order for the Huey to fly, we have to keep a one-gee load on the rotor. If that didn't feel 'normal' to you, that might present difficulties. We'll have to figure that out for the other students."

"It will not be hard," he assured her, flashing a quick grin in her direction before turning his visored face back to look out the windscreen. "We are used to encountering varying gee levels with our other craft. But perhaps it might be useful to install an accelerometer, just so the spinborn may have something concrete to tell them what is acceptable and what is dangerous."

"That's not a bad idea," Mara said. "I'll talk to El and the maintenance team about it."

"I am honored," he said. "But yes, that is part of the reason I wanted to come this way. I know these hills. I spent the first nine years of my life exploring them from top to bottom. Long enough for my bones and musculature to be well established." He thought a moment. "A little too long, actually."

Mara frowned. "Why is that 'too' long?"

Ozendi shrugged. "I should have gone to one of the rohabs—rotational habitats—when I was four or five, but the shuttle sent to pick me up had to be diverted, and it was several additional years before the next one came to this region. So, I came late to living and moving in low- and zero-gee." He smiled. "But as you have seen, I am a swift learner."

"And your body didn't regress once you got there?"

"A little," he said. "But I was already earmarked as a planetary liaison by that time, so I trained very hard to keep my body in condition to return."

"I didn't think you guys had any permanent planetary settlements."

"We do not have settlements, exactly, and those few places that we visit regularly are kept very quiet. I was only authorized to tell you because—because it was necessary for the flight program."

He was going to say something else. Mara didn't know how she knew that, but she did. He had corrected himself and given a different, albeit true, answer. Curiosity burned within her, but she pushed it aside. As much as she wanted to know, there wasn't a reason for her to insist, and to do so could be damaging to the excellent working relationship they'd built.

Because building relationships was their key to survival. Just as the contemporary "Terran" officers had pointed out shortly after awakening her and as Murphy continued to emphasize in all of his communications. Forging those relationships were just as crucial a mission as getting the helicopter training spun up. She couldn't afford to forget that.

Even if it meant that her attraction to Ozendi continued to grow.

She shoved *that* thought aside as well and forced her focus down to her watch and then to the map she held in her gloved hands.

"There should be a distinctive rock outcropping coming up," she said. "A stone spire that's been weathered away from the rest of the cliff. It'll be at your one-o'clock at approximately half a kilometer—"

"Contact," Ozendi said. Mara flicked her eyes up to the windscreen and, sure enough, there it was, a little more than 500 meters away.

"Perfect," she said. "That's our turn point, so keep it out your right door and turn around it. We'll have to climb a little to get through the pass below it."

"Pulling in power to seventy percent torque," Ozendi replied as he approached the landmark. "Right turn...clear right."

Without Elroy in the back to look out the large cabin windows, the pilots had to clear their own turns. Mara had been relentless in her instruction, ensuring that Ozendi developed the discipline to turn his head and look *every time* before he banked the aircraft.

Mara punched her stopwatch button, resetting the leg timer, and glanced at the map again. "Keep your climb at ninety knots if you can, please," she said. "It should only take us a minute and change to clear the pass, and then we'll see the next river valley beyond the ridge. The river is our boundary, so don't cross it. We're looking for what looks like a wide, flat turn in the stream, like the beginning of an oxbow."

"I know the place," Ozendi said. "Leveling off. This should keep us one hundred meters from the highest point in the pass."

"Good," Mara said, looking up again. The terrain really was breathtaking. On either side of their pass, craggy granite peaks rose. Vegetation grew on every slope that wasn't sheer rock, and its dark, cool green-blue colors looked black in the morning shadows. They cruised through the pass and descended down the other side, being careful to keep clear of the uneven terrain as they approached their river valley. This was the last leg of their first flight, the leg that would bring them into the settlement where Ozendi had been born, and where Elroy awaited them now.

* * *

They made it to the settlement, which Mara had already christened "FOB Ozendi" in her head. It consisted of a village with a wooden stockade, perched on the wide bank of the mountain stream they'd followed. Like their training site, there was a large, open field which bore scorch marks from the engines of orbital shuttles, not far from one of the gated entrances.

"I'm guessing our people set up near the same landing field," Mara said, glancing down at the satellite imagery and then back out at the landscape. "Yep. That looks like Sergeant Frazier's vehicle at the northwest corner there. Make your approach to the north end of the field."

"Roger," Ozendi said, easing the collective down and beginning a turn designed to bleed off his airspeed to the point where he could make a safe, controlled approach and landing.

Mara called out his altitude and airspeed as they both decreased, until they wound up in a respectable four-foot hover, about fifty meters from where Elroy waited, leaning on his vehicle, arms and legs crossed. Despite her sudden urge to jump out and hug her battle buddy, Mara made herself sit still and help Ozendi step through the After Landing and Engine Shutdown Checklists in a methodical, disciplined manner. Once the rotor slowed to a stop, Elroy came forward and opened the rear cabin door.

"Good to see you, ma'am, sir," he said as he reached under the left alcove seat for the pelican case that held the rotor tiedown cord, among other things. "I've got fuel on standby, and the village put together a lunch for you guys to take with you. I told them you'd quick turn this afternoon but be back to spend the night this evening."

"You're a godsend," Mara said with relief. "I brought snacks, but I wasn't really excited about them."

"You will like the food, Mara," Ozendi said as he pulled his helmet off and grinned at her. His tousled helmet-hair made him look younger than usual, heaping a boyish appeal on top of his other attractive qualities. "It is full of flavor."

"It's good," Elroy confirmed in his usual laconic fashion. "Naliryiz—she's the Doc—has it all ready for you over by my truck."

"Truck?" Mara asked, raising her eyebrows. Elroy pulled the tiedown free of the box and gave her a shrug and a tiny smile.

"Good a name as any," he said. "Y'all go eat. I'll get your bird fueled and turned."

"Naliryiz is here!" Ozendi stowed his helmet behind his seat, his face splitting in the widest grin Mara had seen from him yet. "I was hoping she would be the one to come!"

"You know her?"

"She is my sister!" He reached down and fumbled at his harness release in his haste to untangle himself and get out of his seat. He pulled the door release, kicked it open, hopped down, and broke into a run toward Elroy's vehicle. Mara watched as a smaller, female-shaped figure emerged and headed toward Ozendi. She didn't run, but she did open her arms wide and allow herself to be caught up in a hug that lifted her feet off the ground. Mara snorted softly through her nose as she undid her harness and stepped out of the vehicle. The man was like a puppy sometimes—all endearing exuberance!

Mara spent a long minute or two putting her helmet on her seat and her flying gloves into her pockets before walking around the nose of the Huey to join her copilot and his sister. She didn't want to intrude on their family reunion, but they were on a bit of a tight timeline if they wanted to get all of their training in today, and she was hungry.

"Mara, please, come meet my sister," Ozendi called out. He turned, leaving one arm around his sister's shoulders, and beckoned to Mara with his free hand. His face lit up with joy, and Mara felt a strange, ugly feeling twisting in her gut. She tamped it down hard, anger at her stupid irrationality erupting in her brain. Of course, the man was happy to see his sister! She'd have given anything to see her own family, wouldn't she?

...and that was another thought best locked away. Mara forced her face into a smile and stuck out her hand as she mentally shoved all of her inconvenient thoughts back behind the steel doors of her mind. "Hello, Doctor," she said, keeping her voice determinedly light and cheerful. "It's nice to meet you."

"You as well, Captain," Naliryiz said, taking Mara's hand in her own. She inclined her head slightly, in the way Mara had seen some of the SpinDog females do as a greeting, and swept her long-lashed eyes closed for a second before returning Mara's frank gaze.

Naliryiz was, to put it mildly, stunningly beautiful. Where her brother looked every bit like a Pacific Island warrior, Naliryiz had a more mystical, ethereal look to her. Part of that was the slender, delicate build of the orbital-born, but there was also something otherworldly about her eyes, with their long, dark lashes and their honey-colored irises. She looked like she could see right into your soul, a thought which made Mara have to fight the urge to squirm.

"Please," Mara said. "Call me Mara. Or 'Bruce,' if you like. It's my callsign. Your brother and I haven't been particularly formal in that way."

"No," Naliryiz said, glancing up at Ozendi, her tone dry. "I can see that. But then you must call me Naliryiz. Or 'Doc,' as your sergeant does."

Some of the tension in Mara's shoulders eased, and she glanced back toward Elroy and the bird with a smile. "He does, doesn't he? You know, that's a compliment, him giving you that title. You must have impressed him."

"I have been made aware of the significance of the nickname," Naliryiz said, her beautiful full lips curving in a smile that sparked through those striking eyes. "I am deeply honored."

"Well, if he trusts you enough to call you 'Doc,' then I do, too. Welcome to the team."

Ozendi looked between the two women, confusion twisting his face. "I do not understand," he said.

Naliryiz looked at Mara, but Mara just raised her eyebrows and tilted her head slightly, indicating that the other woman should go ahead and explain.

"On their world," Naliryiz said, "the warrior caste is but a small part of their society. Those who perform healing arts are not generally part of that caste...except for those who are. When one of their warriors calls a healer 'Doc,' it means they honor the warrior within the healer, and they trust the healer to stand beside them in the face of the enemy, if necessary."

Ozendi frowned at his sister. "Sergeant Frazier does not trust easily."

"No," Nailiyiz said, "he does not. But one of their team members suffered acutely during planetary entry, due in part to some past trauma, I believe. I treated the man as soon as we landed yesterday, and Sergeant Frazier was grateful. He began calling me Doc after that."

"What are y'all doing standing here jaw-jacking?" Elroy asked, his deep voice threaded with exasperation. Mara turned to see the big man approaching from where she'd left him at the aircraft. "The bird's got full bags, ma'am. You need to eat and move out if you're gonna meet your timeline."

"Thanks for the reminder, El," she said. "He's right. Shall we?"

"This way," Naliryiz said, gesturing. She turned and led them to the vehicle, now much dirtier than it had been when Mara had last seen Elroy driving it away through the trees.

The big man walked up to it and slapped the front fender affectionately. "This truck ain't a bad rig at all," he said. "She made steady progress through the nastiest terrain. Not the most comfortable ride I've had in my life, but I've had worse, too. And she's got plenty of cargo room."

Mara followed Ozendi and Naliryiz to the rear of the vehicle and saw that Elroy was right. There was ample space for two large, nondescript containers in the back. Naliryiz opened one to reveal a stack of local fruits, a container of something that looked like pine-nuts, and two covered bowls. She reached inside and handed one of these to Mara, and the other one to Ozendi.

Mara watched Ozendi and followed his movements as he pulled the cover—a type of close-woven fabric Mara had never seen before—off. He bent over the bowl and inhaled deeply, pleasure writ large on his face.

"Delicious," he said. "Did you make this, my sister?"

"Iope did," Naliryiz replied softly. Because Mara was watching Ozendi for clues on how she was to eat this dish, she didn't miss the slight tensing of his eyebrows, the deepening of the corners of his mouth at his sister's answer.

"Ah. She's a wonderful cook," he said then, his voice clear of any tension. He turned to Mara and grinned. "This is *debem*. Roasted grain, meat, and local vegetables with spices. You must try it!"

"Use your hands," Elroy supplied quietly behind her. "Like rice and fish."

Mara smiled her thanks at him and reached into her bowl. She had to admit that the contents smelled wonderful: savory with heat and a hint of sweetness. She grasped a portion with her fingers and put it into her mouth, trying not to drop any down the front of her flight suit.

Flavor exploded into her mouth. Heat kissed the surface of her tongue, mingled with salt and a deep meatiness that made her eyes go wide with pleasure. She chewed slowly, experiencing the texture as well as the taste.

"Wow," she said after she swallowed. "This is amazing."

Naliryiz's smile grew and, for the first time, she directed it fully at Mara. "I am pleased you like it! *Debem* has many ingredients that will be beneficial for you. I think you will not need to eat again until you return to us tonight. But you will take these *leob* fruits and roasted seeds just in case."

Mara might have doubted at first, but as she continued to eat, she realized the dish was, in fact, extremely filling. As she used her fingers to sweep the last bits out of the bowl, she found herself full, but not uncomfortably so, and she had to admit that Naliryiz could very well be right. The food was in every way superior to her own stash of dry crackers and spreadable cheese.

"We need to go," she reminded Ozendi as she followed his example and wiped her hands clean on the cloth that had covered her bowl.

"Yes," he said, excitement in his voice. "I am ready. Thank you, my sister," he said, and hugged Naliryiz hard with one arm. The slight healer returned the embrace, and, once again, Mara felt a stab of envy. Though whether it was for the closeness of a sibling or for Ozendi's obvious affection, she couldn't have said. Rather than think too hard about it, she turned to Elroy.

"You're all ready to go," he said. "I'll be here waiting for you when you land. We've got billets set up, and you can meet the rest of the team tomorrow morning. There's a call scheduled with Murphy tomorrow night."

"Sounds good," she said, smiling. "Take care of everyone here."

"Yes, ma'am," he said. "Don't let the SpinDog kill you."

"Fiiine. I promise." She sighed, rolling her eyes in mock exasperation. Elroy snorted softly and gave her a tiny grin. She winked at him and turned to walk back to the bird, her mood restored from its momentary dip. It was time to get back in the air.

* * * * *

Chapter Three

Their route initially continued to follow the river as it wound through the mountains and out toward the southern plains. The sun—which was hard to think of as the binary system's "secondary"—angled toward the west as they flew, beams slanting through the terrain and gilding everything below. Mara had taken the controls, giving Ozendi a break and a chance to practice his navigation. She reveled in the feeling of flying as she banked the Huey at a forty-five-degree angle toward a ridge, using the aircraft's energy state to make the climb up and over.

"Continue down and to the left," Ozendi instructed, glancing down at the map. She looked out her left window in response and then turned the aircraft further in that direction.

"Clear left," she announced as the Huey responded to her touch. After so many flight hours, the helicopter was like an extension of her body. She didn't have to think about the mechanics of balancing her cyclic, collective, and pedal inputs anymore. She merely thought *down and left*, and the Huey responded.

"We're going to follow this valley for several kilometers—"

Plink. Plink plink plink…

"Mara! What is that?" Ozendi's voice on the intercom cut through the sudden, high-pitched scream of the number one engine.

Mara ignored him. She knew what it was.

"Breaking right! Ground fire, ten o'clock!" she said crisply as old training kicked in. She whipped the cyclic to the right, and saw the fire light on the number one engine flash orange against the darkness of the dash. She slammed the collective halfway to the floor and dove for the dubious protection of the trees. As she turned, she glanced down to see what looked like a camp hidden in the trees below. A camp with several vehicles mounted with weapons. Weapons that were shooting at them.

"Engine fire in number one!" Ozendi shouted. "I smell smoke!" He started to reach his hand toward the warning light and the handle that, if pulled, would shut down that engine.

"Wait!" Mara ordered into the intercom as she banked back to the left, initiating a momentary climb that would hopefully make them harder to track. A bend in the ridge further to the left held a promise of safety, if she could get the Huey there in time. "She's still giving me power! Let her burn, we gotta get out of the WEZ!"

"Mara! More muzzle-flashes! They're still shooting!"

Mara buried the nose and pulled up on the collective. The scream from the number one engine intensified, and the acrid scent of smoke began teasing into her nostrils. She saw the bend in the ridge draw closer, and she whipped the bird further to the left to put the rock outcropping between the Huey and those determined to take her down. They carved through the air around the terrain and into another narrow mountain valley. Less than a hundred meters below, a tributary stream bubbled over rocks and fallen trees as it flowed to join the river.

She waited for a three count and then eased back on the collective to slow their airspeed into the range that would allow them to fly on only one engine.

"Okay," she said, forcing her voice to be calm, collected. There was no time for emotions. "Boldface. Now."

Together, she and Ozendi did the boldface steps of the emergency checklist by memory, shutting down the number one engine and activating the engine fire extinguisher. The warning light winked out, which made her draw in a deep, shaky breath of relief.

"All right," she said then. "Get the checklist. Let's clean this up and see what we've got."

To his credit, Ozendi had regained his composure and situational awareness, and he had the checklist ready to go. In truth, Mara couldn't fault him for losing it momentarily. Everyone reacted differently to being shot at, and almost no one held it together the first time.

"Power, checked," Ozendi read.

"Roger," Mara said. "You watch the engine gauges; I'll keep an eye on the rotor and the torque. We should have right at fifty percent available."

"Roger," Ozendi echoed. "Copilot is posted on the engine gauges."

"Power's coming in," Mara said, and she began a slow, steady pull of the collective. The number two torque needle rose in response, climbing through thirty percent, forty…

"Stop pull! Number two engine temperature is at maximum!"

"Shit," Mara said, glancing down at the stack of engine gauges to confirm it was true. Sure enough, the number two engine temperature gauge showed the needle right at the red line. Even worse, as she watched, the oil pressure in the number two engine began to decrease at a slow, but steady, rate. "They must have hit number two as well. We're going to have to land."

"Can we fly it back to the settlement?" Ozendi asked, though the sick tone of his voice indicated he already knew the answer.

"I don't think we've got that much time," Mara said. "The oil pressure is already at the minimum. I know it'll run for a little while if it pisses all the oil out, but if it comes apart, it's gonna be ugly. I think we'll have a better chance if we shut it down on our terms and make a safe autorotation."

"Okay," Ozendi said. "Okay. Let me see—" he looked down at the map, and then back up again. "Yes! I know where we are. There is a plateau ahead, into which this stream spills as a small cascade. The plateau is a flood plain. Mostly flat and very wide, without a lot of trees. It is a good space for autos."

Privately, Mara thought that nowhere other than a prepared runway constituted "a good space for autos," but she didn't think saying so would be particularly helpful. Instead she concentrated on flying at sixty knots; that airspeed would give her the maximum rate of climb. Or it should.

It also occurred to her that whoever had shot at them was still somewhere out beyond their six, but that thought was even less helpful at the moment, so she pushed it away and kept flying.

Below them, the mountain stream twisted and turned, cutting through the rocks on either side. It was probably only a minute or two, but it felt like hours before Mara spotted the waterfall ahead.

"There it is!" Ozendi said, the joy in his tone making it clear that he, too, had been anxious.

"Okay," Mara said. "The winds are pretty calm, so I'm just going to shoot this along the longest axis, which is probably going to be parallel with the stream, right?"

"Mostly," Ozendi said.

"Good enough. I've managed to eke out a little more altitude for us, so I'm gonna trade that for some extra airspeed and try to enter this thing as close to ninety knots as possible. I want to make it look as much like what we practiced as I can, all right? As soon as I enter and roll the throttle to flight idle, I want you to shut the engine down, okay? Get that throttle off so I'm not trying to reengage it at the bottom. Don't worry about the pilot not flying calls, I'll make them for myself. Got it?"

"Got it," Ozendi confirmed, and a tiny corner of Mara's mind laughed to hear him solemnly repeat the Earth-born slang phrase.

Mara eased the cyclic forward, pulling in power right to forty percent, and willed the aircraft to accelerate. The airspeed needle crept around the dial, slowly reaching first seventy knots, then eighty…

"Over the falls now," Ozendi said, his voice calm.

"Roger," Mara said, keeping her own voice empty of emotion. "This is real world, crew. Entering in three…two…one. Autorotate. Throttles Flight Idle."

As she spoke the words, Mara slammed the collective to the floor and rolled the number two throttle all the way back to the idle stop. The speed with which she'd lowered the collective helped to spike her rotor speed, which was what she wanted. She felt the throttle move beneath her hand as Ozendi toggled the idle stop release and rolled the twist grip throttle all the way off, shutting the engine down. It got eerily quiet after that, with only the whine of the rotor in the background.

"Two hundred feet," Ozendi said, reading off the radar altimeter. Mara's eyes flicked through her crosscheck, looking first at her rotor speed, then her airspeed, then her trim ball, then glancing outside to her intended landing area. It loomed before them, and only Mara's discipline and years of habit patterns kept her from getting sucked into staring at the ground rushing toward them.

"One fifty," Ozendi said.

Rotor. Airspeed. Trim. Outside...

"One hundred feet. Flare, flare, flare."

As Ozendi made the flare call, Mara pulled back on the cyclic, a little bit at first, and then gradually more and more as she progressively bled her airspeed off and converted that energy into rotor speed. She could hear the whine of the rotor increase in pitch, and she gritted her teeth and forced herself not to pull up on the collective to correct it. This was for real. She wanted all the rotor energy she could get.

"Hold it off," she whispered to herself. "Hold it off..." She kept holding the cyclic aft until it felt like they were about to slide backward onto the Huey's tail, and then she exhaled and let off the cyclic pressure. The nose started to fall back toward the horizon, and Mara glanced at her attitude indicator to make sure she brought the helicopter all the way to a level position.

And with her left hand, she pulled.

She held her breath and pulled upward in as smooth and steady a movement as she could manage. She pulled and kept pulling, forcing the Huey's rotor to use all of the energy she'd shoved at it to cushion their landing as the skids touched down on crack-webbed mud of what looked like a dry lakebed. The rotor noise changed in pitch; the scream became a moan as she converted all of the rotor speed into lift.

The Huey skidded forward for a few feet, bouncing slightly, before shuddering to a stop and rocking first forward, then aft on the skids. Above them, the rotor swooped once, twice, slow enough for Mara to look up through the greenhouse and see the individual blades in turn. On the master caution panel in front of them, several lights blazed, showing that the engines were, in fact, no longer working.

But they'd done it.

Mara drew in a deep shuddering breath and closed her eyes. For just a moment, the memory of her son's face flashed behind her eyelids, and she pressed her lips together to keep from crying. Her hands shook. Everything shook.

"You did it!"

Ozendi's triumphant tone jolted Mara out of her daze. Her eyes snapped open, and she took another breath.

"We did it," she said on the intercom, pleased to hear her voice as steady and calm as before. "I'm gonna do an emergency shutdown. We're not on fire anymore, so you stay put. We probably spread the skids a little bit, and I don't want the rotor taking your head off."

Her hands flew over the switches required to shut down the remaining systems on the aircraft. Once the rotor was stopped and the battery off, she reached up and removed her helmet, hoping that Ozendi couldn't see the tremor that remained in her hands.

"Well," she said brightly, hoping it sounded like she was joking. "I got us here. Your turn; what's next?"

* * *

It turned out Mara already knew what was next. Once the blades had slowed to a stop and she'd shut everything down, she and Ozendi got out of the aircraft and took stock.

"Well, she's fucked six ways from Wednesday," Mara said, disgust and anger mingling in her tone as she looked up at the charred ruin of her number one engine. "How does number two look?" "The cowling is glowing red," Ozendi called to her from the other side of the aircraft. "I can't open it to take a look." "Awesome," Mara said. "Well, okay. We knew we weren't flying out of here anyway, so I guess this doesn't change anything. Lucky for us, Murphy just sent down a full maintenance response team. If we can get them out here, they might be able to figure out how to salvage her...if we knew where 'here' was, that is."

Ozendi appeared at the nose of the aircraft. "I know where we are," he said, a slightly distracted frown creasing his features.

Mara blinked, then stared at him. "You do?"

"Of course. Remember, I told you I grew up in these mountains. That's how I knew about this flat space where the creek floods in the winter."

"That's right!" Mara said. All of a sudden, she remembered the satellite imagery they'd been using for navigation. She lunged for the cockpit door, leaned in, and pulled the crinkled pages from the map holder on the copilot's side.

"Here," she said, shoving the maps at him. "Can you mark our location on this map?"

"I can," he said. But his voice held doubt, and his frown deepened as he met her eyes. "But Mara, I don't think I should. I know our location, and how to get back to the settlement...but those people who shot at us..."

"Yeah, who were those assholes?" she asked, anger further jacking up the jittery adrenaline dump skittering along her nerves. "I thought the indigenous R'Baku didn't have modern firearms technology."

"Most do not. And those who have it do not reveal or use it lightly."

"So, who—?"

"I do not think those who attacked us are R'Baku. I am not certain, but I fear that they may be raiders from Jrar. If they find us or these maps…"

Mara froze at this unexpected answer. Unable to help herself, she glanced over her right shoulder at R'Bak's slowly setting sun, profoundly orange as it sank toward the horizon.

"Raiders?" she asked softly. "Do you mean a scout team? Like the ones who were stopped by my people when we arrived? Or have the Searing culls come early?"

"One of those. I know not which. What I do know is that they *cannot* be allowed to find our settlement!" Intensity throbbed through his tone, and his dark eyes went hard with controlled horror.

"Yeah," she said. "With my people there, I can see how that would be bad. Okay then, this is out of my realm of experience. What do you think we should do?"

Ozendi shook his head and shoved a hand through his sweat-matted hair. "It's not just that. The settlement itself—" He broke off, shook his head again, then appeared to force himself to focus on her question. "We must get back as quickly as possible. There is a wood-cutter's road from the settlement that passes near here, but I am hesitant to use it."

"Yeah, if they're looking for us, we should stay away from roads."

"We should be able to hike out cross-country, but the way is difficult. Sometimes, rock- or mud-slides leave it impassable."

"Then hiking back is what we'll do," Mara said, reaching out her hand to rest it on his forearm. "We'll get what we need from the bird and head that way. We've got a little time before both the sun and the primary set, yes? Let's get as far away as we can and then we'll stop for the night when we find a good spot."

Ozendi nodded. "Yes," he said. "Yes, that is good. That is what we should do."

"All right," Mara said. "Grab your bag, fill it with the fruit and stuff that Naliryiz sent with us. Grab the maps, too, and anything else that's easy to carry in your backpack. Let's keep our hands free if we can. Is that water safe to drink, do you think?"

"It is," Ozendi said. "It comes straight from the ground a day's hike from here."

"Okay, I'll take your word for it," Mara said. "Fill up your water bottle, and we'll get going."

He nodded again, a single, sharp movement of his head, walked past her to slide the cabin door open, and began grabbing his bag. Mara watched him closely for another moment, just to make sure he wasn't *too* tightly controlled, before she walked around to the right side of the aircraft and followed suit. Within a few moments, they had packed up what food they could carry and a few other things, and they were kneeling beside the creek, filling water bottles.

"Oh! One more thing," Mara said. She shrugged her backpack off her shoulders and jogged back to the aircraft. She pulled open the cockpit door and leaned in to remove the tiny key in the side of the center console. She zipped it inside the small pocket on the upper arm of her flight suit and then turned to run back down the bank to Ozendi.

"Ready," she said.

"What did you need?" he asked. He looked so different from her smiling, flirtatious student. This morning, he'd been all flashing grin and easy charm. Now she found a hard determination to succeed.

"The key," she said. "It's a small thing, but at least this way if the assholes find the bird, they won't immediately be able to figure out how to start her. I should have disconnected the battery, too, but it's getting late and we should get going."

"I've always wondered why there was a key, anyway. It serves no other function than to complete the electrical circuit to the starter, right? Why could you not just have a complete circuit without it?"

Mara grinned and slung her backpack up onto her shoulders.

"That's an interesting story," she said. "Lead the way, and I'll tell you while we walk."

Ozendi looked at her, and, for the first time since they'd been fired upon, a ghost of a smile played about his lips. "All right," he said. "This way."

He turned and began following the creek upriver to a spot where it narrowed. Mara shrugged her pack once more, settling it into place, and followed him.

"Once upon a time," she said, "Hueys didn't have ignition key-lock keys. But one night, in a place called Tipton Field, Maryland, a man named Robert Preston decided he was sick of being shit upon, and he was gonna do what made him happy…"

* * *

They didn't get far before both stars set and it got too dark to keep going, but Mara figured progress was progress and tried not to stress about it.

Ozendi hadn't wanted to stop for the night. She couldn't blame him; it had to be hell knowing that the raiders were out there, close to the vulnerable settlement of his people. She could feel the tension singing through him as it got steadily darker under the canopy of the R'Baku polar forest. She'd managed not to say too much, but their progress slowed to a crawl as he peered through the trees, straining to make out the landmarks that would point the way home.

"Ozendi," she said softly. "I think we need to stop. It'll take us longer to get back if we get lost in the darkness."

"I am not lost," he said sharply, almost snapping at her. "I am just making sure. We must just get up and over this ridge..." He trailed off, but kept walking, pushing through the undergrowth. Branches whipped back at her, requiring her to keep one hand raised up to protect her face.

"Ozendi," she said again, a bit more steel in her tone. She stretched her legs in order to push up beside him. "This is stupid. Let's just find a place to cam—"

The ground crumbled beneath her right foot as she stepped down. Mara tried to throw her weight to the left, but it was too late. She felt the slope collapse under her weight as her ankle, and then her knee, buckled. A strangled scream ripped itself from her lips as she tumbled. She tucked her shoulder into a roll and barely managed to keep the back of her head from hitting a fallen tree trunk. Her face hit the forest floor as she spun. Something sharp stabbed her cheek just below her right eye.

"Mara!"

Ozendi's voice followed her down the slope. Mara skidded to a stop against a piled-up mass of tangled branches and needles that had built up next to a largish rock—almost a boulder, really. She groaned and pushed herself over onto her shoulder, then blinked twice to clear the dirt from her eyes.

"Wh-what?" She coughed, spat out some of the dark, R'Baku forest loam, and squinted up the slope in time to see Ozendi stumbling down the hill in patent disregard for his own safety.

"Are you all right?"

"Mostly," she said, spitting again. She grunted and shrugged out of the straps of her backpack, before pushing herself up to a sitting position. Electric pain shot up from her knee and ankle, and she pressed her lips together to keep from screaming. "That fucking hurt."

"I am sorry," he gasped out as he reached her, sending more of the loose dirt and forest detritus up into the air as his feet slid to a stop. He grabbed onto one of the branches in the deadfall and steadied himself before crouching beside her. "I am so sorry. This was my fault."

"Yep," Mara said evenly. "Sure was." She grunted again and hauled her backpack into her lap. She opened the front pocket and began digging for her flashlight. "Help me see how bad the damage is. Nothing feels broken, but my ankle and knee hurt like hell."

Ozendi knelt down and gingerly put his hands on either side of her knee. Despite the lightness of his touch through her flight suit, she winced as pain shot up through her hip. She gritted her teeth and managed to keep from making any sound other than a hiss as he gently felt her leg from thigh to heel. Eventually, she remembered her plan, and her fingers closed around the thick, textured cylinder of the flashlight in her bag. She pulled it out and clicked it on, shining the red light over her leg. No bones or blood. Those were both good signs. Though she could see her knee was starting to swell.

"Well, buddy," she said, her voice rough with pain. "Looks like we're gonna camp after all. I can't go any further on this tonight. Tomorrow, you might have to continue without me, depending on this swelling."

"Do not worry about that," Ozendi said. He laid her leg back on the ground as gently as possible and then stood and grabbed her backpack. "Let's just find a place to shelter for the night. There are predators in these hills."

"Oh? You might have mentioned that before," she said, rather mildly, all things considered.

"They generally do not bother us. But now you are injured and vulnerable."

"Thanks for the reminder."

He turned to look at her, and in the fading light from the suns and the red glow from her flashlight, Mara could see the self-recrimination writ large on his face.

"Mara," he said. "I—"

"Don't worry about it," she said sharply, cutting him off. "That gets us nowhere. Just find us a place to camp and help me get there. Then we'll figure out a plan."

"I—all right," Ozendi said. She watched him square his shoulders slightly and shift his weight as he started to look around. He glanced to the top of the ridge, from where she'd fallen, and then further down the slope. "Wait here. I will return shortly."

"Leave me my backpack," she said. "In case you don't."

He stared at her, and she let herself give him a tiny, dry smile. She wasn't sure if he could see her expression or not, but she smiled anyway. Eventually, he snorted softly and turned to pick his way carefully down the hill.

Darkness continued to rise up from the forest floor while she waited. Mara's knee and ankle began to throb in concert with one another. She concentrated on breathing in and out, drank some water, and continued digging in her bag. She could have sworn she had a small packet of aspirin…

It felt like she waited forever. The forest began to make what she assumed were its usual night sounds. One of the most disconcerting things about R'Bak were the ways in which things felt familiar. She remembered many happy evenings spent listening to the sound of nocturnal birds and insects chirping as she and her family camped out in forests much like this one. For just a moment, she closed her eyes and inhaled deeply, remembering.

Woodsmoke mingling with the scent of roasting meat and burnt pine pitch. The warm weight of her son, laughing in her arms. Sticky marshmallows and chocolate melting over her fingers…

"Mara!"

Ozendi's voice echoed through the alien trees up at her, jolting her back to awareness. She shifted the red light toward the sound and surreptitiously swiped at her eyes with the back of her free hand. Hopefully, it was dark enough that Ozendi wouldn't see muddy tear tracks through the dirt on her face.

"Here," she called, her voice a rough croak. She cleared her throat and tried again. "I'm here. Did you find a spot?"

"Yes," he said as he drew near. In the weak circle of red light, she saw him bend down and reach out his hands to her. "It is not as near as I'd hoped, but it will work well. Can you stand?"

"I think so, if you help me." She reached up and felt his strong fingers wrap around her wrist. With a heave, he levered her up onto her good foot and managed to duck under her arm to support her.

"It's going to be interesting going down the hill like this," she said as they hobbled the few meters necessary to clear the area of deadfall where she'd been sitting.

"Yes," he said. "I thought about that. It's mostly clear right here. If you sit down again, I think we might be able to slide down the slope in a mostly controlled manner."

Mara laughed a little at "mostly controlled," but since she didn't have any better ideas, she reached out to steady herself on a nearby tree trunk and helped him lower her back down to a sitting position. She'd missed the "we" in his sentence, she realized, or she hadn't recognized his intent, so he surprised her by lowering himself to the ground behind her and spreading his legs on either side of hers.

"Keep your feet together," he said in her ear, his breath warm against the side of her neck. "My legs are longer, so I will act as a buffer for any obstacles we encounter."

"This seems like a terrible idea," she said.

"Do you have a better one?"

"I've been trying…but no. Fuck it. Let's do it."

He let out a short, surprised laugh, his chest rumbling against her back. She settled her backpack in her lap and pressed her legs as close to each other as possible, wincing at the fire in her knee and ankle every time she moved.

"Ready?" Ozendi asked. Before she could say yes or no, he pushed off, and they began sliding down the hill, loose forest debris spilling like a wake behind them. Mara fought down nausea from the pain and felt her body tense, readying for the impact that would surely come when they barreled into a tree, or a boulder, or another deadfall, or…

…or nothing, because the slope evened out at the bottom, and they coasted to a gentle stop in the dirt.

"I can't believe how well that worked," Mara said. Ozendi laughed again.

"You might try trusting me more often," he said. "I generally know what I'm doing."

"I fly with you, don't I?" Mara said. "That's trust."

"Yes, but you keep your hands close to the controls at all times."

"Well." Mara shrugged, looking up at him as he got to his feet behind her. "That's practicality." She couldn't see his face in the darkness, but she imagined he was smiling.

"Come," he said, reaching down to take her hands again. "It is not far."

* * *

It wasn't actually that far, for which Mara was intensely grateful.

Ozendi half-carried her a few more meters toward the bottom of the valley and then along the length of it for a minute or two. It felt like an eternity, but eventually he paused next to a place where the valley wall rose up in a sheer cliff.

"There is a small cave back here," he said, his breath coming quickly. "Shine your light on the cliff there."

Mara obliged, and sure enough, she could see a narrow, vertical slit of darkness half obscured by brush.

"That's good," she said. "Nice and hidden. Is it big enough for both of us?"

"Yes," Ozendi said. "Hold on, I will have to carry you." He bent and tightened the arm around her waist, while slipping his other arm beneath her knees. She could tell he was trying his best to be gentle, but pain shot through her at his touch. She pressed her lips together so hard that they hurt, but a muffled sound of distress escaped anyway.

"I am sorry," he said, breathless.

"It's all right," she said. "Just get me there."

Mara tucked her head close to his chest, feeling his warmth radiating through his flight suit beneath her cheek. She felt him duck as he stepped through the narrow cave opening, angling her body so she didn't hit the rock walls. It had been dark outside, but that gloom was nothing compared to the blackness inside the cave. Ozendi took only two steps and then stopped.

"Shine your light," he said. "I want to make sure this is a safe place to put you down."

Mara played her light around them. The dim redness seemed impossibly bright in the full dark as it showed an uneven, undulating wall and a sloping, dirt-covered floor that held nothing but a pile of old bones and branches.

"We are not the first to shelter here, it seems," Ozendi said, his words rumbling through his chest. "But I do not smell anything, so I think the pile is at least a season old. I'm going to put you down now, all right? Then I'll see about making a fire. The cave opens out behind us, so we should have adequate ventilation."

"Is that smart?" Mara asked. "What if it draws the assholes to us?"

"We should be shielded well enough in this cave," he said. "And we could both use a little light and warmth, at least until we sleep."

Since her hands and feet had stopped shivering and gone numb with cold a while ago, Mara didn't argue. She just braced herself for the lancing, stabbing pain as Ozendi bent to set her gently down on the cave floor. She scooted herself backwards so she was leaning against the wall, and then took a moment to congratulate herself for not passing out from the agony as she did so.

She pulled her backpack into her lap and began digging in it for tools and supplies while Ozendi used the piled-up branches to create a small, merry blaze.

"You were right," Mara said softly as the fire crackled in the makeshift pit he'd scratched out of the dirt on the floor. "We did need a fire. I don't know why, but I feel better having one."

"Fire is light and warmth and comfort," Ozendi said, giving her a smile that seemed to flicker in the uncertain light. "We who have spent time planetside crave it on an instinctive level. On the Spins, it is a different story. I have many friends who are not comfortable with fire at all."

"Fire is dangerous in space." Mara nodded. "I get that."

"Do you have those fruits? I will roast some. They're delicious that way."

She held out the bag, and he dug around in it. He grabbed two of the fist-sized fruits and cut them open, then removed the sweet flesh and speared it on the tip of the knife she'd seen him carrying in his pocket.

"The sugar caramelizes with the heat," he said as he held the speared fruit down into the yellow flames. "And the fruit puffs slightly. It's very good. Try it!"

"Like a marshmallow," Mara said as she accepted the offering when he held it out to her. She tossed the hot, sticky mess from hand to hand and then popped it in her mouth, sucking in air to help it cool. It even tasted a little bit like a roasted marshmallow: all crispy, burned sugar. "It's delicious."

"What is a 'marshmallow?'" Ozendi asked as he speared another bit on his knife. "Is it a fruit from your planet?"

"Not a fruit, a candy," she said. "It's basically spun sugar. They're terrible for you, and even worse when roasted. But they're delicious. Donnie used to love them."

"And who is Donnie?" Ozendi asked, a joking edge to his tone. "A lover? A partner you left behind?"

"No," Mara said, her voice going quiet and empty. "My son."

Ozendi inhaled, and Mara could tell he had turned toward her, but she kept her eyes steadfastly on the flames.

"Mara, I am so sorry," Ozendi said. "I did not know you left a child behind."

Mara nodded. "He was four," she said, keeping her voice even. She never talked about Donnie, or much about her old life at all, but all of a sudden, the words seemed to well up inside her, wanting nothing more than to spill out into the flickering firelight of the cave. "His dad and I divorced, but we stayed on good terms. We used to take Donnie camping every summer. He loved to roast marshmallows and make s'mores. He's dead now, I suppose."

"You don't know that," Ozendi said.

Mara let out a harsh laugh. "Yes, I do," she said. "It's been over a hundred years since that…since I entered cryosleep. He's long dead. He was staying with my ex when I was deployed. My ex wasn't a great husband, but he was always a good dad. Sometimes…"

She felt her lips curve up in a smile. "Sometimes I think about Donnie growing up, going to high school, playing sports, having a girlfriend. Stuff like that. I imagine him getting married and having kids. The Army would have given me a funeral and stuff, given him a flag. I like to imagine him telling my grandchildren about me. Showing them the letters I wrote home to him, telling him how much I loved him—"

She broke off when Ozendi's fingers brushed her cheek. Her eyes had flooded again. She sniffled hard and looked down in embarrassment.

"Sorry," she mumbled.

"Do not be," Ozendi said, his voice rough. "Do not apologize. You are so hard, so strong, all the time. You can…you are allowed to hurt for this."

His words broke the dam. Mara squeezed her eyes tight against the flood and opened her mouth in a scream. Grief swelled within her, pressing out from the center of her skull, from the core of her chest. She pulled her arms inward, crossing them over her heart, her fingers curled in claws of agony as she finally opened the door on the thoughts she'd been pushing aside since she first woke in the Dornaani infirmary, since before she even met Murphy.

Wave after wave of grief and memory washed over her, paralyzing her as she gasped, choking in the dark on pain and loss.

She wound up lying on her side, the stone floor of the cave cool under her cheek. Her knee and ankle throbbed abominably, but her physical discomfort had faded to background noise under the on-slaught of the emotional maelstrom. Firelight flickered, painting mobile shadows across the tiny space. Mara sniffed and tried once more to wipe her eyes.

"What I wouldn't give for a shower," she muttered, her voice rough but even as she pushed herself up to a seated position. She felt empty, wrung out, as if the explosion of emotion had burned her clean from the inside out.

"Here," Ozendi said. He reached into his own pack and pulled out what looked like a spare T-shirt. He shook it open and then wet it with some of the water in his bottle. "There are many streams and springs around here," he said, holding the damp cloth out to her. "At least you can wipe your face and hands."

"Thank you," she said. She hoped he understood she wasn't just talking about the cloth. She took it and immediately began scrubbing her face.

"May I look at your leg now?" Ozendi said. "I'm not as good as Naliryiz, but I might be able to help a little."

"Sure," Mara said. She sniffled mightily and straightened the leg as best she could. He came forward and gently prodded at her knee and ankle. "I don't want to take the boot off," Mara said as his long fingers felt around her foot. "I can already feel it swelling, and I'm afraid I won't get it back on."

"It is fine," Ozendi said, his voice pitched to be reassuring. "You will not need to remove it, I don't think. I think you are right; nothing feels broken. This is good news; I have something in my pack to help with swelling and inflammation."

He turned to rummage in his bag again while Mara continued to wipe her face and hands free of the clinging grit. It wasn't the shower she longed for, but she had to admit that she felt better once she was done. Ozendi turned back to her just as she was folding up the cloth.

"Here," he said, holding up a small fabric twist. "This is what I was looking for."

"What is it?" Mara asked, unable to keep her tone entirely free of suspicion.

Ozendi laughed. "Just herbs. A local blend. You dissolve them in your drink. Naliryiz makes this for the liaisons because we're naturally clumsy when we first come back to planetary gravity. It will reduce the swelling and the pain."

Mara eyed the packet with distrust, but since she didn't have a flight doc handy and she really needed to be able to walk tomorrow, she gave a short nod and held out her water bottle. Ozendi opened up the packet and carefully poured in the powdered mixture. Mara capped it and shook. The whole thing turned a muddy, unappetizing brown color in the firelight.

"Down the hatch," she muttered as she uncapped it and chugged. To her surprise, it didn't taste bad. It had a sort of citrusy zing, but mostly it tasted like the scent of newly mown grass. She'd definitely tasted worse.

"That should work quickly," he said. "I think you will feel much better tomorrow."

"Let's hope so," she said quietly, suddenly feeling very exposed. She looked away from him, staring steadfastly at the fire.

"Mara." Ozendi's voice was soft, and he bent close until she had no choice but to make eye contact. "You are all right. Grief is to be expected in your situation. Have you not allowed yourself to mourn yet?"

Mara shrugged one shoulder and looked away again. "It's just easier, you know? Especially with the guys. I'm secure in my position and stuff, but it's never good for them to see a woman crying. They tend to think we're weak. I can't believe I let you see."

"You know I do not fault you. Many among my people think as you do. But living on R'Bak for so long when I was young, I saw that for people like you, the problem is not weakness. Your problem is that you have been too strong for too long. One thing I have learned from my travels in both worlds is that emotions must be felt, Mara. Otherwise, they fester like a wound untreated."

She looked back at him, and his nearness shivered along her skin. "Not every emotion is a smart emotion," she whispered. He quirked the corner of his beautiful lips in a tiny smile and reached out to brush a stray piece of her hair behind her ear.

"We are talking of emotions, not logic. Smart or stupid doesn't apply."

"Maybe not, but they do apply to behaviors. Choices. It isn't smart for me to choose to let the guys see me crying."

"It isn't smart for you to lock your emotions away indefinitely, either." His fingers traced her cheekbone. "You have to deal with them eventually."

"When it's safe," Mara murmured.

"It's safe," he assured her and leaned in. His lips hovered a breath above hers. She could feel the almost electric warmth of his skin. "Yes?" he asked.

She shouldn't. There were a thousand reasons why she shouldn't. But none of that mattered in the flickering light and her sudden, agonizing need for touch, for life.

"Yes," she said, and claimed his lips for her own.

Lightning tingled below her skin as he carefully pulled her close. She reached, her hands frantic, and began unfastening his jacket, opening up his flight suit. She nearly ripped his undershirt in her haste to get to him, to feel that warm bronze silk so delicious against her own skin.

"Stars and ancestors, Mara," he groaned next to her ear. "I cannot stop. I cannot get enough of you."

"Then don't," she said, her breath a gasp of need. "Don't ever stop."

Firelight and shadows danced over their bodies as they tangled one with the other, reaching for the knowledge—the proof—that they still lived. Together, they spiraled toward an aching, almost painful climax that left them breathless, holding onto each other like shipwreck survivors clinging to driftwood.

"You—are you hurt?" Ozendi asked, his words broken as he gasped for air.

"No," Mara said, her voice just as breathy. She could feel the languor that followed sex start to seep in, gilding the edges of her thoughts. "No, not at all." She started to roll away from him, but he tightened his hold and pulled her gently, inexorably back, until she lay stretched upon him once more, her head pillowed in the hollow of his shoulder.

"I don't usually cuddle, after," she said, putting some humor in her tone.

"What is your English expression? Oh, right. Shut the fuck up, Mara."

She stiffened, unsure whether to laugh or be insulted. He went on, his hand playing idly with her hair.

"I know what you are doing. You are trying to put me—this—in a box with all of the other things you don't want to feel. But now that we have come together, I have a say, too. I won't let you lock me away, Mara. You feel this, the same as me."

"I just thought—"

"That is the problem. By the mercy unknown to the Death-fathers, Mara. Stop *thinking.*" He stroked his fingers over her shoulder, down her back to her hip, and back up, trailing fire under her skin with his touch. "Just let me love you."

"Love?"

"Shhh," he said and stopped her mouth with a soft, hungry kiss. "You're thinking again. Is not this love? You desired me, and I you. And now we've come together in beauty and pleasure and need. What else would you call it?" he whispered when he was done.

"This is just sex. Love is—I don't—"

"Is not sex a form of love? Just as friendship is love? Loyalty is love? I think perhaps you have been so angry at yourself for waking up that you have severed yourself from all of these things. You deserve to feel, Mara. You deserve to be loved."

She should have gotten angry. She knew that. She should have shoved him away and told him that her feelings were none of his business. She should have threatened him with bodily harm if he touched her ever again...

But he was touching her now, and igniting that need that still slumbered within her, and she wanted...oh, she *wanted* him. All of him. Not just his beautiful warrior's body, but she wanted everything else he was saying. She wanted his laughing eyes and his sweet smiles and his inside jokes. She wanted his presence beside her, bolstering her nerve. She wanted his strength to augment her own. She wanted his words whispered in her ear.

She wanted him. She wanted to feel. She wanted his love.

And she was so, so tired of fighting what she wanted.

"And you," she whispered, hating the vulnerability in her voice, but knowing it needed to be there. "You…want to love me?"

"I have since the first time we flew together," he said. "Since the first time I glimpsed the real you behind the façade of toughness you wear so well."

"Okay," she said.

"Okay?"

"Okay. I want you. To love me."

"Then I shall, I promise."

She felt his hand glide once more down over the curve of her hip. He lifted her, pulled her more fully atop him, and stared up into her eyes. Then he smiled.

And did.

* * * * *

Chapter Four

Dawn filtered through the cave, waking them. Mara felt good, despite not sleeping for most of the night. The herbal remedy seemed to have significantly improved her knee and ankle, and she took a couple of experimental steps, carefully allowing it to take her weight.

"How do you feel?" Ozendi asked. He had extinguished the banked fire and was busy repacking the items they'd pulled out during the night.

"Really good," Mara said, surprise threading through her tone. She turned to him with a grin. "Not nearly as tired as I would have expected."

"There are many forms of rest," he said and gave her an exaggerated wink. She threw her head back and laughed.

"Where did you learn to do that?" she asked. "Is that something your people do?"

"No," he said. "But I have seen your people do it from time to time. Did I get the context wrong?"

"You nailed it," she said, and walked over to him with just the barest trace of a limp. As she'd hoped, he opened his arms to welcome her into an embrace, and she took a moment to breathe in his scent and revel in the replete soreness she felt from the previous night's exertions. Ozendi wrapped his arms around her and held her close.

"Since we are speaking of your people," he said, "do you think there will be trouble for you, because of our connection?"

"Murphy will be pissed," Mara predicted, a grim edge forming around her words. "But he'll get over it. In the end, what can they do to me? I'm one of our few pilots and *the only* one with quals on more modern birds. They need my skills too badly to put me back on ice." At least, she seriously hoped so.

"I will help protect you if I can," Ozendi promised. "There will be no repercussions to me for taking you as a mate. Especially if…well, my people will protect you if necessary."

"I think it'll be fine," Mara said and dropped her arms. "But that's a problem for another day. For now, we need to get back to the settlement and let them know about the raiders…and figure out how to get my maintenance team back to our bird."

Ozendi let her go and smiled down at her as she stepped back.

"I did not feel like you would welcome this before, but I feel that I should tell you: you are quite arousing when you take command."

Mara snorted. "Well, I hope you've got some extra room in your shorts, buddy, because this is who I am."

"Oh, I am very aware," Ozendi said with a satisfied smirk. Which made Mara laugh again.

They started out in high spirits. The day itself seemed to echo Mara's sunny mood back to her. The sunlight streamed golden and green through the trees, and though Ozendi set a brisk pace, it wasn't nearly as punishing as it had been last night. Mara's knee and ankle continued to improve as they walked, too.

"Damn," she said as they stopped near another one of the innumerable mountain streams to refill their water. "Whatever that herb cocktail is, I need to get some. My ankle doesn't hurt at all, and my knee only twinges when we're going up the steepest grades."

"Naliryiz may make some for you," he said. "It works very well and is very safe. Only—well, you will have to ask her about it. I do not know if she will want to share it with all of your people."

"Why not? A secret recipe or something like that?"

"Something like that," he said. She let the matter drop.

The journey took them the rest of the day. They took a short break around midday, stopping to eat and rest for a little bit. They made love again under the spreading limbs of the blue-green forest, while the dual suns heated the air around them in a soundless promise of the Searing to come. By the time the suns dipped below the western horizon, they were nearing the top of another great ridge.

"The settlement is just on the other side," Ozendi said. "Though it will take another hour or so to reach it. Will you walk in with me?"

Mara looked up sharply at the sudden vulnerability in his voice.

"What do you mean?" she asked.

"I mean, I know that you said there could be some trouble for you…"

She shook her head. "Let's worry about that later. We don't have to say anything when we first get there, we've got other priorities. But yes, I will walk in beside you, and if people draw conclusions, they can draw conclusions. Hell, they probably would have anyway."

He smiled, though his eyes seemed troubled, but he said no more. He simply resumed hiking up the slope toward the top of the ridge.

Once they got to the top, Mara smelled smoke.

"Cookfires," Ozendi said when she asked. "Nothing to worry about." But he picked up the pace just a little bit anyway. Once again, Mara mentally thanked the absent Naliryiz for her concoction as she hitched up her pack and followed Ozendi down the slope, into the night-dark valley.

* * *

Darkness blanketed the settlement. Mara tasted the acrid tang of smoke in the back of her throat as they threaded through the trees along the river toward the stockade. No firelight—or any kind of light, for that matter—penetrated the smoky gloom.

"Ozendi," Mara said, pitching her voice low. "Something's wrong. There are no fires."

Ozendi nodded but didn't say anything. Mara pushed aside a wistful thought that they should have armed up before setting out yesterday and followed close on his heels. She was right at his shoulder as they broke through the screen of forest and looked at what remained of the settlement where he'd been born.

The stockade was mostly left standing, though it smoldered in quite a few spots. Thick smoke billowed up from the center of the town, blotting out the star-encrusted sky as it rose.

"Dio," Ozendi whispered, and broke into a run. A tiny corner of Mara's mind wondered who had taught him Spanish, but she ignored that and took off after him as he pelted through the stockade's gates. They looked as if they'd been hit by something heavy, for they swung, splintered, on battered, warped hinges.

The town inside was dark, too, and seemed deserted. Fear opened up in a pit in Mara's stomach. Where were her people? Where were *any* of the people?

Ozendi ran all the way past the center of town toward a place near the rear wall of the stockade. He stopped dead in front of a smoking pile of wood and rubble and stared, his face pale in the darkness, his eyes open holes of pain and denial.

"Ozendi."

Mara whirled at the sound of the woman's voice, her hand going for the small knife she held. Fire flared in the darkness, and relief flooded through Mara as the newly lit torch revealed Naliryiz's symmetrical features marred by grief.

"Doc!" Mara called out. "Ozendi, look! It's your sister! She's all right!"

Ozendi turned and lunged toward Naliryiz. He wrapped her up in a tight embrace, heedless of the torch she held. As quickly as he'd grabbed her, though, he let go, and stepped back, holding her by the shoulders and peering into her face, his own ravaged by grief and worry and...rage?

"Iope and Dio were alive, the last I saw," Naliryiz said quickly, her voice quiet and even. "They were taken, along with several others."

"Who?" Ozendi asked, though Mara was pretty sure they already knew the answer.

"Raiders," Naliryiz said. "Early and too far north, but they looked and acted like the advance parties we've seen before."

"Were my people taken?" Mara asked.

Naliryiz shook her head. "No," she said. "They joined with our resistance and fought the raiders off. They were most helpful. But Kelrevis was taken, as well."

"I know where they took them." Ozendi said, his voice icy cold but still throbbing with urgency. "We can get them back."

"Wait," Mara said. "Hold on. We'll get them back, Ozendi, but you can't just go barreling in there. Let's take a breath; make a plan!"

"You don't understand!" he snapped at her. Then he shook his head abruptly and let go of his sister's shoulders and stalked away, his chest heaving as he fought to breathe.

Naliryiz looked after him, and then offered Mara a small, half-smile.

"Forgive him," she said. "You are right, of course, and he knows it. Iope is his mate, Dio is Diozera, his daughter, and Kelrevis is one of our matriarchs. This is a terrible blow. His agony is understandable just now."

Mara blinked at Naliryiz as the healer's words registered.

Iope is his mate. Diozera his daughter.

His mate.

His daughter.

An image rose up in her mind's eye, unbidden. Ozendi laughing, his eyes dark with passion as he spoke to her of love. Mara closed her eyes and shoved the image away, pushed it into the box where she'd sworn it would never go and locked it down behind every mental barrier she held.

"Where are my people?" Mara asked, forcing her eyes open, her voice to be calm.

"We have set up a field hospital in your landing area. Many were hurt. Everyone has gathered there."

She should have gone to him. Mara knew that. But in that moment, she just couldn't.

"Bring him when he's ready. Tell him we'll get them back." As she spoke those clipped words, Mara saw Naliryiz's eyebrows furrow. Doubtless, she wondered why Mara was being so cold. But Mara couldn't do anything about that, any more than she could stop the anguished, tearing feeling inside of her.

One problem at a time.

She nodded sharply to Naliryiz and turned away. Let the healer see to her brother. Mara would find Elroy, find her people, and find a way to get her lover's family back.

Even as it broke her heart.

* * *

"I understand your position, Captain, but the rest of the task force isn't ready to deploy planetside yet. And if it was, it is far too early for us to show our hand."

Mara glared at the static-blurred shape of Murphy's face and fought the urge to spew profanity. She inhaled slowly through her nose, and then exhaled before nodding her head once.

"Fine," she said. "Then given the *strategic imperative* of our mission here, I request permission to take command and do it my damn self!"

Murphy glared right back at her, and Mara could feel his icy fury radiating down the lines of the comm link. She didn't care. Let him freeze her out. The rage boiling inside her was hot enough to melt any ice he threw her way.

"Agreed," he said more readily than she expected, but his words were still clipped. "We must provide assistance, but you should send your student instead, Bruce. Your abilities are far more strategically important than—"

"Ending the call. Enemy could triangulate and locate." She cut the connection before he could complete the order for her to sit this one out. Like hell she was sending Ozendi in to rescue his family and the rest of the villagers without her. He was too distraught. He'd never make it out alive. Truth be told, she would have preferred to leave him out of it altogether, but she needed his local knowledge to get back to the Huey and find the raiders' camp.

She sighed and stepped back, then turned to find Elroy watching her from just inside the flap of the tent where they'd set up the comm set.

"You okay?" he asked, his voice a soft rumble.

"I'm fine," she said, and made to step around him and out of the tent. He moved to the side, and she came up hard against the iron muscle of his chest.

"Don't lie to me, Bruce," he said, using her callsign as he only did in private. "Something happened between you two out in the woods. You won't even look at the guy. Did he hurt you?"

Mara surprised herself with a hacking, joyless laugh.

"No, El," she said. "He didn't try to rape me. I swear, you fucking men think that's the end-all, be-all of 'bad things that can happen to a woman!' Besides, do you think he'd still be breathing if he had?"

"No," Elroy admitted. "Okay, fine. So, what *did* happen?"

She wasn't going to tell him. She had absolutely no intention of telling her 6'5", Vietnam-era badass of a crew chief about her broken heart. But when she drew in a breath, the words tumbled out all over themselves anyway.

"He said he loved me," she whispered. "He told me I deserved to be loved and that he wanted me always, and then I come back here to find he has a family. God! I'm so fucking stupid! Listen to me, I sound like a teenage girl!"

"You sound like a woman who's been hurt," Elroy said, and he reached out and gently pulled her into an embrace. Mara drew in a deep, shuddering breath, and tears of rage and agony started to fall. Elroy held her close, the rock to her storm, and supported her while she let all of her whirling, tangling, distracting emotions out.

"Fucker is right about one thing, though," Elroy said once her maelstrom quieted. She sniffled mightily and swiped at her eyes, then leaned back to look up into his ebony face.

"What's that?" she asked.

"You do deserve to be loved, Bruce. You hold people too much at a distance. This group we're with...well, we're all we've got, now.

It's like being in the bush in 'Nam. You can't push people away because you're gonna need them. Eventually."

An uncomfortable thought wormed its way through Mara's mind.

"El?" she asked softly. "Do you—I mean, have I—"

Elroy laughed and dropped his arms from around her. "Nah," he said. "Don't worry, I'm not much into white women. Too dangerous for a young black man where I grew up. We're a crew, though. And I love you like my sister."

Relief washed over her, and she hugged him briefly before letting go again. "I love you, too, El," she said. "And I'm proud to call you my brother."

"See?" he said, white teeth flashing in a grin. "That wasn't so hard, was it? Do you want me to kill him?"

"Who? Ozendi??"

She felt him nod and knew his offer was 100% serious.

"No."

"All right. If you change your mind, just say the word."

She sniffled hard again and wiped her eyes, then her nose with her sleeve. "When this is over," she said softly, stopping him as he turned toward the tent flap. He looked back at her and she forced her shoulders to relax. "When this is over, if you're willing, I'd love to tell you about my son. Donnie."

Elroy smiled a slow smile, sympathy dark in his eyes. "I'd be honored, sis," he said. "When this is over."

"Right," she said. "When it's over. Right now, let's go kick the shit out of some raiders."

"Amen and hallelujah."

* * *

By the time Mara had her maintenance team assembled and briefed, Ozendi had rounded up a sizeable crew of fighters and vehicles willing to take part in the crazy mission to get their loved ones back. Mara told herself she shouldn't be surprised. The man was obviously capable of compartmentalizing things in his head.

Just as she was.

At one point, while they were planning and gathering resources, he ran to join her as she walked briskly from the field hospital to the vehicle staging point.

"Mara," he said as he caught up to her. He reached out to catch her fingers. His voice was rough. "Mara, please. I must talk to you."

Mara stopped and pulled her hand back as if his touch had burned her. On some level, it had.

"No," she said, her voice cool iron. "I don't think you must. In fact, it's best if you don't."

"But—"

"One problem at a time." She cut him off, turning the corners of her mouth up in a humorless mockery of a smile. "You want your mate and kid back safely, right? Then stay out of my way and let me concentrate on the mission, Copilot."

He just looked at her, pain in his eyes. She felt her internal self yearning toward him, so she did the only thing she could. She turned on her heel and walked back the way she'd come. She would check on the vehicles later.

In the end, they pulled together eight of them. They were the same rugged tracked vehicles Elroy had lovingly dubbed "trucks." Mara's maintenance team had two pairs of M60D machine guns that were intended to be mounted in the Huey's doors. Some genius had figured out how to rig a pintle mount for two of the trucks, and so one of the pairs of weapons was re-purposed for ground use.

Mara had debriefed Elroy extensively on the damage to the Huey, and he and the maintenance team had packed accordingly. Thanks to the extra engine parts they were bringing along, it would be a tight fit in the vehicles, so most of the fighters elected to ride on top, like Mara had seen old soldiers do in WWII films.

By the end of the second day, they were ready to go, furnished with the bare bones of a plan. Basically, they would convoy through the forest to the plateau where they'd left the Huey. This time, rather than going up and down all the ridges, they would take the woodcutter's road and trust to their firepower and speed to get them there safely.

So that was the plan. Mount up and haul ass under cover of darkness. Fix the Huey during the light of day, then assault the raider camp with the bird providing overhead cover. As plans went, it wasn't the most detailed. Or the most survivable. But it was what they had. The twin suns set behind the western ridge, one large disk and one very small, as she and the maintenance team loaded up with Ozendi and his fighters and moved out down the tiny woodcutter's road into the forest.

She rode with Elroy in the center vehicle, the one carrying the majority of the Huey parts they'd need. Ozendi was somewhere else in the convoy. She didn't know where and wouldn't allow herself to think about it.

"Did you talk to the Doc?" she asked Elroy as they crested the first ridge and headed down the other side. They were about an hour into their journey, and Mara was fighting to keep from letting the steady vibration of the vehicle's motor lull her to sleep.

"Yeah," Elroy said with a little smile. "She's gonna take the survivors back to where we set up our school. It's the best option around here for a population that size, and we can easily fortify it with our equipment when we get back."

98 | KACEY EZELL

"If we get back," she groused.

"*When*, sis. Knock it off with them negative waves."

Mara snorted and let the corner of her mouth lift in a smile. Her father had been a big *Kelly's Heroes* fan when she was growing up, so she recognized what would have been a contemporary pop culture reference for Elroy. Instead of replying, she sat back against the crate carrying her new compressor section and pulled out the wrapped bowl of *debem* Naliryiz had pushed into her hands before they left.

"You dig that stuff, huh?" Elroy asked.

"Mmmhmm," Mara said. "It's delicious. Better than anything else I've tasted here."

"Yeah, it ain't bad," he agreed. "I'd kill for a pepperoni pizza, though."

Mara nodded in agreement. "We should try to make one, after this. Pizza's basically just flatbread with cheese and stuff on it."

"Where're you gonna get tomato sauce?"

"Dunno. Ask the Doc most likely. Some of the native stuff might be close. They've got good shit here, El. Ozendi gave me this…tea, I guess you'd call it. I twisted my ankle and knee when we were hiking out; it healed it right up. No swelling at all. And no side effects."

"That you can tell."

Mara shrugged to concede the point. "That I can tell. Still though, it's good stuff. Our medics should take a look at it. They could learn a lot from the Doc."

Elroy shook his head. "She won't teach them. I already asked. She'll treat us, but she won't teach our guys and won't say why."

"Huh. Weird. Maybe some superstition? Like how they don't like AI?"

"Maybe. Who knows, maybe your flight school will soften things up and make them more inclined to share."

"That's what Murphy wants," Mara said. "That's our whole mission here. It's less about teaching them to fly as it is about *forming relationships.*" She couldn't entirely keep the bitterness out of her tone.

"Well, we're doing our best," Elroy said, and reached over to squeeze her shoulder gently. She nodded and focused on eating. She'd need the strength for the night and day to come.

* * *

The bad news was the whole number one engine needed to be replaced.

The good news was they'd brought the parts to do it.

The repair was going to take all day, and that was if they really jobbed it, so Mara did her best to help by staying the hell out of the way. She and Ozendi gathered with his fighters to plan their assault on the raider camp while Elroy supervised the work on the Huey.

Their biggest problem was a lack of basic intel. They didn't know where the prisoners were being held, but from what Mara could remember, the camp wasn't very big, and there didn't seem to be a lot of places for them to stash the almost twenty people they'd snatched from the village.

"I'm betting they're keeping them outside," Mara said as she and the fighters went over her maps of the camp's location. "Probably in a stockade of some kind. We'll be overhead as a gun platform, and I'll relay down to you guys on your handhelds."

One of the fighters shifted uncomfortably at the idea of using the handheld FM radios, but Mara had informed them they had no choice. She understood why they were so careful with stray radio signatures, but with this op being such a last-minute, cobbled-together, jerry-rigged clusterfuck of an affair, they *had* to have reliable, flexible comms. Otherwise, it was a suicide mission, and none of their families would get out.

Truth was, Mara still had her doubts on that score, but she buried them deep and kept going. Because how could she not?

She also mostly-successfully avoided talking to Ozendi about anything personal. She saw him watching her, pain in his eyes. She could feel how he wanted to pull her aside and address the gulf that yawned between them, but he didn't. It was a wise choice, all things considered. Several times during that day, she looked up to see Elroy watching her, as well. Once he jerked his head toward Ozendi and raised his eyebrows in a question. Mara gave him a little headshake, and El shrugged and turned back to his work. She let out a long breath, closed her eyes, and massaged her temples.

Sound drifted over from the work area surrounding the Huey. A flow of guitar notes intertwined with an eerie, winding voice spiraling, singing a wordlessly haunting melodic line. The scratch of a maraca...then the drums stepped in, and Mara recognized a song she'd listened to as a kid and loved all her life.

"What is that music?" Ozendi asked, looking up from the group huddled around the map. Mara couldn't help herself, a grin split her face for the first time since they'd found the burning wreckage of the settlement.

"It's 'Gimme Shelter.'" She tossed the answer back to him without looking as she strode toward the helicopter. "It's a classic Huey song."

The maintenance team was crawling all over the Huey, most of them singing Jagger's lyrics or tapping their tools to the beat on the cowling. Even Elroy was grooving along, swaying his hips as he peered into the now-empty engine compartment.

"Where did you guys get this?" Mara asked.

"Bobby fixed it up," Elroy said, pointing to their avionics tech who was working on the center console, wiring in one of the FM radios they'd brought.

"Bobby?" Mara asked.

"Hey, ma'am," he said, looking up. He had a shock of white-blonde hair and a wide, toothy smile. "I had an 8-track player in my bag when I got snatched. I figured since the bird had a psyops rig for the loudspeaker, and I was in here anyway, I'd hook it up and give the guys a treat. I've only got the one tape, though. Hope these guys like the Stones."

"I think your odds are good," she said. "Thanks for doing that, man. Can you leave it wired in?"

He grinned at her. "Sure thing, ma'am. Gonna do a little psyops?"

"Can't hurt, right?"

"Damn straight."

"This is perfect, Bobby, thanks. Good work."

Mara stepped back from the skid and looked up at Elroy again. "Got an ETIC?"

"What? English, ma'am. I don't speak your future shit."

She sighed, but her smile remained, thanks to the music thrumming through her. "When are you gonna be done?"

"Couple more hours. We should be ready for a test flight before sunset."

"Sounds good," Mara said. "Keep going."

* * * * *

Chapter Five

Thanks to the heroic efforts of her maintenance team, the Huey was once again flying by sunset. They did a quick check-out flight then landed back on the plateau. They'd brought a little extra fuel in their convoy out, but they didn't want to waste gas, so Mara shut her down and waited for full dark.

Six of the trucks had left at sunset, carrying the local fighters. They'd follow the woodcutters' roads and game trails to a spot upslope from the camp where they could wait unobserved. It would take them an hour or two to get there. By the time they were ready, it would be dark enough for Mara to come in low and fast over the treeline.

Their plan was incredibly simple. Mara would kick off the op by flying in and opening fire from the air. Then the trucks would roll in, hopefully vectored by intel from Mara and Ozendi, snatch up the prisoners, and roll out again while Mara continued to keep the raiders' heads down. Elroy and another MACV-SOG guy named "Bones" would be her gunners. She and Ozendi would fly. The guys on the maintenance team that hadn't gone ahead to join the party would head back to the settlement in the two remaining trucks and hopefully meet up with the convoy on their way out.

It could work.

Probably.

"You ready, sis?"

103

104 | KACEY EZELL

Elroy's deep, rumbling voice cut through the fog of her wool-gathering, and Mara blinked as the cockpit of the Huey came back into focus.

"Yeah," she said, reaching up to pull her helmet off its hook and pull it on. "Just thinking it through."

"Well, it's time to stop thinking and start doing," Elroy said over the intercom. "Bobby just transmitted they're in place."

"Roger," she said. "Scramble Checklist."

Ozendi responded with the appropriate checklist steps, and soon they had the bird in the air, armed to the teeth, and flying south. Moonlit trees and terrain blended into a blur as Mara focused on the task at hand: get in, lay down covering fire for the trucks, get out again.

Five minutes from the camp, Mara made a short transmission to the ground team. She got a single break in squelch as a reply, but that told her all she needed to know. The trucks knew she was overhead, and they were rolling.

"Game time, gentlemen," Mara said, her voice icy calm over the beat of the rotor. "The camp is just on the other side of this ridge. Left gun, right gun, call out anything that looks like it might be our people, all right? And if anyone shoots at us, light them the fuck up."

"Roger, ma'am," Bones said, and she could hear the sound of him charging his weapon through the intercom. Elroy did the same on his side but said nothing.

"Up and to the right," Ozendi said, turning his head to clear in that direction before applying power and banking the Huey. They crested the ridge at an angle, in a bank, so they had multiple options if they took fire on the other side.

"Camp is at the ten o'clock, low," Mara called out, reaching for the cyclic and collective. "IP has the controls." She rolled out of the bank, but continued their descent to the level of the trees and kept her nose buried so they would pick up as much speed as possible.

"I got eyes on the convoy," Bones called out behind her. "Back at the eight. Coming in hot."

"Copilot's contact with the prisoners," Ozendi said, his voice professionally blank. "A pen next to the river at the far edge of camp."

"Left's contact, too," Elroy said.

"Excellent," Mara said. "Vector them in, Copilot. Bones, keep me apprised of the trucks' progress," she added as Ozendi toggled the floor mike and made the transmission to their ground team.

"Let's wake them up, boys," Mara said. She reached overhead and toggled the loudspeaker switch on and hit "Play" on the 8-track player Bobby had strapped to the dash. Immediately, the cascade of notes began falling from the Huey's external speakers, starting up the haunting, twisting melody once again.

"I've got enemy gun trucks in parking on the left," Elroy called out.

"Cleared hot," Mara said, and her crew chief opened up with the thick, snapping bursts characteristic of the M60. Mara felt the floor of the Huey shudder as he methodically walked his fire down the line of parked enemy vehicles. Charlie Watts' drum line kicked in right as lights flared inside the makeshift tents and temporary buildings of the camp.

"I've got the friendlies," Bones said. "They're approaching the pen with the prisoners."

"Roger," Mara said. "Keep any enemies clear of that area."

"You got it." She heard answering snaps from his direction, though they broke off as the aircraft approached the line of friendly trucks barreling down on the objective: a rough animal pen half-filled with scared-faced people. From the quick look Mara got as they roared overhead, most of them looked to be female or very young.

"Targets down," Elroy said as an explosion boomed out, lighting up the sky and blinding Mara for a breathless instant. She blinked furiously and waited for her vision to come back.

"Hard left turn," she announced as soon as she could see again. Bones quit firing and cleared her turn. She pulled back on the cyclic, then banked hard over, using her anti-torque pedals to assist her through the turn. This brought the nose first up, then quickly back down and around as the bird whipped through 180-degrees to come back around toward the bulk of the now very awake enemy camp.

"Left gun, right gun, cleared to fire," she announced again as they passed over the convoy of friendly trucks now pulling up to the pen and starting to load prisoners inside. She could see enemy figures emerging from tents and other parked vehicles, weapons out and pointing at them, but Bones and Elroy continued their steady rates of fire, and as soon as the enemy muzzles came up, the fighters went down under the torrents of 7.62 x 51 mm FMJ streaming down from the Huey's two M60s.

"Climbing right turn, Spooky pattern," she called out, pulling in power to both climb and accelerate as she started a steady spiral up and to the right. Bones ceased firing and began calling out the convoy's progress. Elroy continued raining hate down onto the camp as they flew a circle all the way around it.

"Status?" Ozendi demanded over the FM radio. The radio squawked a burst of static. Then the hurried words "Halfway there" came through.

"Shit! I'm out!" Elroy said over the intercom. Mara immediately turned right, away from the enemy, and whipped the bird around into a left-hand orbit. On the loudspeaker, "Gimme Shelter" faded out and the first rhythmic beats of "Paint it Black" echoed through the night.

"Right gun, cleared to fire!" Mara said, her voice still empty and cold as she re-established the Spooky pattern overhead.

"Last truck's loaded!" Bobby's voice over the radio sounded loud and breathless, and unaccountably clear. "Moving out!"

"We'll give them one more orbit—" Mara was saying, when Ozendi suddenly swore and grabbed at the controls.

"Mara!" he said, panic slicing through his tone. "I see Diozera! In the village! Cease Fire! Cease Fire! That's my daughter, nine o'clock low!"

"Fuck! Left gun's visual! She's in the center of the village, in that cleared area with the torches."

"My controls!" Mara said, her tone losing all its ice and cutting through the intercom like a scorching blade. "Bones, call me on the approach!"

She didn't think. She just moved. Afterward, Mara couldn't have recounted what she did with the controls, but somehow, she brought the Huey screaming down on an approach punctuated by Bones' defensive fire that set them squarely in the middle of the enemy camp...

...where a tiny girl crouched, huddled next to the shot-up hulk of one of the enemy vehicles.

"Dio!" Ozendi screamed. He clawed at his harness restraints and had the door open almost before Mara had the skids fully on the ground.

"El!" Mara demanded.

"I'm on him," Elroy replied, and she heard his intercom disconnect as he hopped out behind her copilot, his personal .45 in his hand. The two men ran to the little girl, who knelt with her face in the dust, her hair whipping around her as she pressed tiny hands over her ears. Mara watched, refusing to feel anything at all as Ozendi lifted his daughter, held her close, then handed her to Elroy before turning and running for a nearby makeshift building.

"Shit! Where the hell's he going?" Bones asked.

"I don't know," Mara said. "Here comes El, help him with the baby."

In front of the nose, Elroy curled over the girl and ran, hunched low, toward the bird. When he reached the open cabin door, Mara turned to look back and see him place the kid—she looked like she was about four years old—on the floor of the Huey.

"Mama and one more are being held inside! He's going after them!" Elroy shouted without hooking his comms back up. Mara barely heard him over the beat of the rotor.

"Go get him!" she yelled back, waving her hand to urge him on. *"Hurry!"*

Elroy gave her a short, single nod, and took off running toward the same building.

"Get the kid secured," Mara ordered Bones.

"Already done," he replied, his voice as calm as ever. "We got company incoming."

"Keep them off us for as long as you can," she said. "El just got to the building."

"You got it, ma'am," the old Vietnam vet said. Under his words, Mara could hear the *pop pop* of enemy fire. Little puffs rose up from the dust, working toward them. Bones answered with another burst from his M60. "If I don't get a chance to tell you, you're a helluva pilot, ma'am."

"Thanks, Bones," she said. "Here they come!"

Sure enough, Elroy and Ozendi appeared, each of them carrying a woman. The one in Ozendi's arms had long, blonde hair that almost brushed the ground. The other one looked older, thin and frail as her head lolled against Elroy's chest. Both women looked bloody and battered to within an inch of their lives.

Someone else's problem, Mara reminded herself. *You gotta get us out of here.*

The track changed again, and Jagger's voice started asking permission to introduce himself as more gunshots rang out, this time from the right side of the aircraft. Elroy flinched and crouched lower, then turned and fired his .45, hunching to protect his burden with his body. Ozendi stutter-stepped, and then slowly toppled forward.

"FUCK!" Mara shouted. *"EL!"*

There was no way under the twin alien suns that Elroy could have ever heard her. Not with the gunfire and the rotor wash and the chaos. But he looked up at her anyway, and when she stabbed her finger toward Ozendi's fallen form, Mara could see a jolt go through him.

Elroy didn't bother with niceties. He took the two steps necessary to get to the bird and half-threw the old woman into the cabin. Then he turned back, crouching and running to Ozendi's crumpled form. While Bones let loose with all the covering fire he could muster, Elroy grabbed the copilot's collar with one hand and got the other under the woman's arms and hauled them the last ten feet toward the Huey, even as Mara heard the *plink plink plink* of shots hitting her fuselage.

"They're in!" Bones said. "El's got the door closed on their side!"

"Don't let them fall out!" Mara warned. "We're off!"

The Huey screamed as she pulled right to her maximum power and shoved the nose over to take off straight ahead. Bones' weapon continued to snap in double-time as she turned to keep the left side of the aircraft pointed at the enemy while she ran, hard, for cover.

Mara dove for the little stream that cut alongside the camp, twisted and turned along its path to present as difficult a firing solution as possible.

"Here they come!" Elroy said, his voice ragged and breathless, but back on the intercom. "Shit, I thought we got most of their vehicles. There's at least five coming after us, two with vehicle mounts."

"Hang on," Mara said grimly, as she put the nose down even further, descending closer to the water, and pouring on the speed. Up ahead, the terrain flattened out, offering her even less in the way of options and cover.

We're not going to make it.

"Bruce! Do you need help?"

The voice came in over the FM radio, staticky and thick with a Russian accent. Mara looked up just in time to see a Hind scream by overhead, releasing its 83mm rockets.

"Hind got 'em!" Elroy cried out, jubilant. "The gun trucks are down!"

Tears of joy threatened to swamp Mara, and she couldn't keep the grin off her face or out of her voice as she keyed the mic and spoke to her two fellow helicopter pilots.

"'Bout time you got here, Sergei!" she said. "Your timing is perfect!"

"You know me," Sergei, the senior Russian helicopter pilot said. "I promise I never miss party!" In the background of his transmission, she could hear the Hind's powerful 23mm gun hammering away at the pursuing enemy forces.

"Yeah," Mara said, laughing as tears ran unheeded down her face. She eased the collective out and started a gradual climb, no longer afraid to silhouette herself against the night sky. "I know, you promised."

* * *

"Elroy, how we looking back there?" Mara asked as they crested the ridge and started back down. She forced herself to keep her eyes looking outside the aircraft, no matter how badly she wanted to turn around and see what was going on in the cabin.

"I've got the baby, ma'am," Bones said. "El's doing CPR on the mama. The old lady's breathing and conscious, but barely."

"And the copilot?" she forced herself to ask. Forced herself to keep her voice empty. Forced herself not to think of his name, lest she start screaming.

Bones didn't answer.

"Bones?"

"I'm sorry, ma'am," the gunner's gravelly voice went soft, broken. "He didn't make it."

Mara pressed her lips together and swallowed hard.

"Roger," she made herself say. And then she didn't say anything more until after they landed.

* * * * *

Chapter Six

Mara radioed ahead. Doc Naliryiz and a team of folks wearing medical masks were waiting for them at the headlight-illuminated landing field. She maneuvered the Huey to land as softly as possible, shut it down, and then waited for all of her passengers, dead and wounded alike, to be unloaded. Then, and only then, did she unfasten her harness and ease herself out of the seat.

The adrenaline rush from the firefight had long since worn off. Fatigue pulled at the edges of her mind, crushed her body under its weight. She carefully gathered up her gear and walked slowly back through the beams of the headlights toward the operations building.

Elroy found her in the locker room, crumpled against the far wall, sobbing so hard she couldn't breathe.

To his credit, he didn't say anything. Instead, the MACV-SOG warrior just walked over and picked her up, cradling her close. For the second time in three nights, Mara screamed silently as a storm of rage and grief ripped through her, scouring her insides with the acid torrent of regret.

Gone.

He's gone.

And there was nothing she could do about it.

Eventually, though, the storm quieted. Mara found herself half-lying across Elroy's lap, his iron-hard arms holding her securely against him. She could feel his chest rumbling as he hummed a wordless tune.

"What is that?" she whispered, her words ragged and raw.

"Hmm? Oh, nothin'. Just a song my mama used to sing to us boys when we's little if we had a bad dream."

"I wish this were a bad dream," she said.

"I know, sis. Believe me, I know."

"He wanted to talk to me. I wouldn't let him."

"I know."

"I was so angry at him. And now he's dead. And I'll never know what he wanted to say."

Mara felt Elroy straighten just slightly, as if something important had just occurred to him.

"Actually," he said slowly, "you might."

"What?" she asked. She felt like Elroy's words should have made her angry, but after her crying jag, she just felt empty. And exhausted.

"I forgot when I saw you on the floor, but I came in here to find you for the Doc. She said she had a message to give to you."

"Naliryiz?"

"Yeah. I told her she should wait, but she insisted you had to come as soon as you were able."

As soon as she was able? Mara was pretty sure that didn't mean "after crying your eyes out for twenty minutes"—or however long it had been. But was she able now?

"I guess," she found herself saying.

"You guess what?"

"I guess I'm able. Let's go find the Doc."

"You got it, sis."

Elroy helped her to stand and finish putting her gear away, then watched her closely as she walked toward the door. Her legs shook like Jell-O at first, but eventually she steadied and moved with a reasonable fraction of her usual purpose.

It's a good thing it's dark, Mara thought as they stepped out of the operations building and headed toward the field hospital which had spread out from the back of the local "alchemist's" house. *I must look like reheated shit.*

They found Naliryiz in the front area of the hospital, addressing several people. Mara recognized two of them as Lawless medics, but the others seemed to be SpinDogs. It hadn't been her intent to interrupt, but Naliryiz broke off as soon as she and Elroy walked into the tent.

"Mara," the doc said, her eyes dark with sympathy. It hit Mara like a hammer blow. *She knows.*

She must have tensed, because Naliryiz immediately turned and dismissed the gathered medical personnel before beckoning to Mara to follow her. Elroy fell in behind them, his expression promising violence to anyone who dared to tell him otherwise.

Naliryiz preceded them down a dimly lit canvased walkway that led to the back of the alchemist's shop. Immediately inside and to the right was a door, half ajar. Immediately across from it, almost fully hidden in shadow, a SpinDog with a weird-looking bullpup carbine eyed them dispassionately.

"We can talk in here," said Naliryiz, gesturing toward the door. "The matriarch may still be awake."

Mara pushed the door open further and stepped inside, to see that the old woman was, indeed, awake and sitting up in a surprisingly advanced hospital bed. She looked up at Mara's entrance and a strange expression—relief? satisfaction?—flickered through her eyes before fading into something that looked very much like a serene poker face.

"Have you told her?" the matriarch asked, looking behind Mara at Naliryiz.

"No, Breedmother," Naliryiz said. "Not yet."

"Told me what?" Mara asked, a shadow of impatience creeping into her exhausted tone.

"There are many things you need to know, child," the matriarch said. "I will ask your patience so that we may explain them in such a way as to make the most sense to you." Her words and expression were kind, but Mara could feel the edge of command in the woman's words. She wasn't used to being gainsaid.

"First, I must ask you a question. I know that you and Ozendi coupled. Are you yet fertile? Is there a chance for a child?"

"I—*what?*" Mara gasped, real anger finally stirring deep within her brain.

"Mara," Naliryiz murmured, her tone half placation, half pleading. She reached out and put a hand on Mara's forearm. "Please. We're not trying to hurt you."

Mara stared at the old, battered woman lying in the hospital bed. The woman stared back, her dark eyes calm and bold and...hopeful?

It was that tiny bit of hope that did it. Mara let out a breath and felt her nascent anger slip away. "There is a chance," she admitted. "I'm not twenty anymore, but...there is a chance."

The matriarch closed her eyes briefly and let out a breath, murmuring soft words of thanksgiving. Then she opened her eyes and smiled a brilliant smile that made Mara's heart ache.

It was Ozendi's smile.

"You must understand," the matriarch said, "forming a romantic partnership with you was never explicitly part of Ozendi's mission. Like you and your *Sko'Belm* Murphy, we *hoped* that a strong working relationship would result, that is all. But when Ozendi contacted us and told us that he wanted to approach you about coming here he confided in me that he felt very drawn to you. He named you 'Skydreamer,' although that isn't exactly right since you are not a planetary native."

"What is a 'Skydreamer?'" Mara asked.

"That is what we call the native people who interact with our liaisons. It gives them a measure of protection, of legal standing within both our society and theirs. *You* already had legal standing as our ally, so the fact that Ozendi felt it necessary to name you thus meant he wanted very much to be with you."

"Is Iope a Skydreamer, then?" Mara said, and try as she might, she wasn't quite able to keep the bitterness out of her voice.

The matriarch smiled, and Naliryiz came forward to take Mara's hand.

"My brother handled this badly," Naliryiz said, her voice soft with regret. "When you returned from the forest, he told me that he never got the chance to tell you about Iope or Diozera. Yes, Iope is a Skydreamer, and she was Ozendi's mate almost three years ago. But you have to understand, Mara, he was no longer romantically involved with her. They loved each other only as Diozera's parents, not as partners for one another."

Grief wrapped around Mara's throat. "You mean—"

"My brother told me he offered to love you, and you accepted. That meant he was yours until his last breath."

Mara bit her lip, hard enough that the copper taste of blood seeped onto her tongue.

"There is more," the matriarch said, drawing Mara's attention back to her. "Naliryiz says that the woman Iope is gravely injured and will likely not survive the morning. She has asked that the two of you—the two women Ozendi loved most—be allowed to take responsibility for the child Diozera. This is a lifetime commitment among our people, Mara. You must think carefully before agreeing."

A memory flashed behind her eyes: Ozendi, explaining his people's customs of caring for one another's loved ones. Her eyes began to burn with regret and loss. She blinked back the tears and straightened her spine.

"I accept," she said, forcing her voice to be as steady and strong as her raw throat would allow. "I know what it means, and I accept. Diozera will be as my own daughter."

"And...if you are with child—"

Mara held up a hand. "Listen," she said, "whether I'm with child or not, you need to understand one thing: I will *never* be parted from a child of mine again. Not ever. So, whether we're talking about Diozera or my own hypothetical baby, that is how it is."

The matriarch's smile grew slightly colder, but it did grow. "That is how we feel as well. These children will form the bridge between our people, Captain. And such a bridge must be unbreakable, unburnable."

Mara stared down the old woman, willing her to see the depth of Mara's commitment. "Breedmother," she said. "I give you my word as a mother. I promise to live up to my part of our agreement." Naliryiz squeezed her hand.

The old woman spoke once more, her eyes closing. "Just as we will live up to our promises to you."

* * * * *

Epilogue

"I read the report. I'm sorry about your...your student, Captain," Murphy said several beats after Mara finally fell silent.

"Thank you, sir," she said, her voice empty. She felt wrung out, as if she'd just experienced it all over again. She looked down and realized that she'd placed her hand on her abdomen without meaning to do so. She forced it back down by her side.

"I seem to recall reading that the child did make it, though. I take it that's the girl you recently brought to the Spin habitat for the first time?"

"Diozera, yes. Her mother, Iope, lived long enough to personally and formally request that we—me and Doc Naliryiz—look after her Dio."

Murphy leaned forward, his elbows on the tabletop. Mara risked a glance up and found not his usual coldness, but something like sympathy in his striking eyes.

"That's what you said. But why would she do that?" he asked. "You never met her before she was taken, correct?"

"That's correct, sir," Mara said. "But..." She trailed off, then squared her shoulders and took a deep breath before plunging on. "You're familiar with the SpinDog concept of Skydreamers, right? The native R'Baku who interface with the Spin liaisons? Ozendi's mother was one. The settlement that was attacked was one of a few places planetside where the offspring of the relationships between a

119

SpinDog liaison and the indigenous R'Baku are raised. Ozendi grew up there."

"One of several?" Murphy asked, his eyebrows climbing his forehead. "There are so many of these children?"

"It's not exactly encouraged," Mara said. "But it's not exactly *discouraged* either. You gotta remember, sir, these people are so very invested in their genetics, right? They know they need fresh genetic material every few generations or so to keep their bloodlines strong. And you've said it yourself, humans are human. Relationships are *going* to happen. Claiming the offspring just allows the SpinDog matriarchs to keep it a little more under their control."

Murphy grew quiet, his eyes boring into hers. "That still doesn't answer my question. Naliryiz is the child's aunt; I understand why she was made responsible for Diozera. Why you?"

"Because," Mara said, "her father loved me. And I'm carrying Ozendi's child." She lifted her chin and met his steely stare with her own. For a long moment, nothing moved. The only sound was the whoosh of air through the life support system overhead.

"Ah," Murphy said softly. "So, you *are* pregnant. I'd wondered if that was why you elected to assume a command and control role rather than fly in the upcoming mission."

"That's part of it," Mara admitted. "The SpinDogs' routine pathogen scan confirmed the presence of embryonic development when I returned from planetside. It's so early I didn't want to risk flying in combat. Although I do believe that I would be useful controlling our air assets."

"I'm sure you will be," Murphy said. "I would have thought that the father might be Sergeant Frazier, or even Vat, though I suppose that's not terribly likely."

"Vat's a friend, and El's my crew chief and brother, but I don't mind if people think the baby is his. It might be easier that way."

"Who among our people knows the child's parentage besides myself?"

"El does," Mara said. "That's it."

"And you think the matriarchs will try to claim your child as they do the children of the Skydreamers?"

"I do," Mara said. "In fact, they already have. It was almost the last thing the matriarch said to me before she died. And *that* is why I know that they will play their part. Because I've made it very clear that this child is *mine*. If they want access to him or her they need to meet their end of any bargains they make with me and my people. You gave me this job in part because I'm good at understanding and analyzing cultures, right, sir? Well, here's my analysis: In the eyes of the SpinDogs, when Ozendi gave me his seed, that was an irrevocable act. We're now as married as two Mormons just leaving the Temple."

"And so they'll play their part."

"They will, sir. I've bet the lives of *both* my children on it." Once again, their gazes met, and this time, Murphy was the first to soften.

"All right," he said. "I believe you. Will you reveal your unborn child's parentage, eventually?"

"Maybe," she said. "For now, I'll just remind anyone who asks that it's not their fucking business…unless it is. Like with you, sir."

"If that's how you want to handle it," he said. "I'd appreciate being kept apprised of your medical status, please. I realize that's not a typical request, but you've managed to set yourself up as the first real bridge we have with these people, and so—"

"Understood, sir," she said. "Both Doc Naliryiz and Doc Arthur say that everything's just as it should be."

He raised a single eyebrow. "How much could they know? It's only been, what, about eight weeks?"

"It's actually shorter, sir; those eight weeks are made up of eighteen-hour days. So more like six weeks, in terms of actual clock time. But the SpinDog Matriarchs are way ahead of us when it comes to prenatal medicine."

"Glad to hear that you are in such good hands," Murphy said, sitting back in his chair. "One more thing, Bruce, before you go."

"Yes, sir?"

"You did well on that mission. I told you that before. Under other circumstances, I would say mounting the assault so quickly was hasty. But given the tactical situation, which I didn't fully understand at the time, you made the right call. Not just to save lives and rescue an important leader, but to demonstrate that our people were ready to risk themselves to save SpinDogs and what they hold dear. I realize you had our strategic goals in mind the entire time. I want you to know that I see that."

Mara swallowed past the sudden thickness in her throat.

"Thank you, sir," she said. "I appreciate that."

"And, Mara…"

"Yes, sir?"

"I am very, very sorry for your loss."

Mara inhaled through her nose and fought to keep her hands by her sides. Grief welled up inside her, threatening to come crashing down like a tsunami. She pressed her lips together and pushed it back—not forever, just temporarily. She gave Murphy a soft smile and got to her feet.

"Thank you, sir," she said. "I appreciate that, too."

"You haven't taken any time. If you need to—"

"No, sir," she said, shaking her head. "I'm fine. Work helps."

"All right," Murphy said. "But please remember, you're not alone. We're here for what you need. It's dangerous to bottle up grief."

Her smile grew, even as she willed her eyes not to fill. "Yes, sir; that's good advice." When she was sure they would not spill over, she added, "Seems like I've heard those words somewhere before."

\# \# \# \# \#

ABOUT THE AUTHOR

Kacey Ezell is an active duty USAF instructor pilot with 2500+ hours in the UH-1N Huey and Mi-171 helicopters. When not teaching young pilots to beat the air into submission, she writes sci-fi/fantasy/horror/noir/alternate history fiction. Her first novel, MINDS OF MEN, was a Dragon Award Finalist for Best Alternate History. She's contributed to multiple Baen anthologies and has twice been selected for inclusion in the Year's Best Military and Adventure Science Fiction compilation. In 2018, her story "Family Over Blood" won the Year's Best Military and Adventure Science Fiction Readers' Choice Award. In addition to writing for Baen, she has published several novels and short stories with independent publisher Chris Kennedy Publishing. She is married with two daughters. You can find out more and join her mailing list at www.kaceyezell.net.

* * * * *

The Caine Riordan Universe

The Caine Riordan series and Terran Republic universe deliver gritty yet doggedly optimistic hard scifi in a world that is a believable and embattled successor to our own. For those who are not familiar with the series' hallmark blend of exploration, alien encounters, intrigue, and action, you can find them all right here:

The **Caine Riordan** series
(Baen Books)
Fire with Fire
Trial by Fire
Raising Caine
Caine's Mutiny
Marque of Caine
Endangered Species (forthcoming)

The **Murphy's Lawless** series
Shakes
Obligations
Man-Eater
Promises
Pearl (coming July 20, 2020)
Waveoff (coming August 13, 2020)

Other works in the **Terran Republic** universe
Lost Signals (Ring of Fire Press)

Since that list includes a winner of the Compton Crook Award, four Nebula finalists, and ten Dragon Award finalists, they're not hard to find. Just go wherever books are sold. Want to learn more about the Caine Riordan series? Easy. Contact any of the publishers, or you can reach out to me at contact@charlesegannon.com.

Want to see more of what's going on in the Terran Republic universe? Check out http://www.charlesegannon.com for exclusive written and visual content.

And if you decide you don't want to miss a single new release or announcement, then go to http://charlesegannon.com/wp/sign-up/ to join the all-inclusive mailing list for sneak peeks, special offers, and features you won't see anywhere else.

And most important of all…welcome aboard; we're glad you're here!

The following is an

Excerpt from Book One of The Psyche of War:

Minds of Men

Kacey Ezell

Available from Theogony Books

eBook, Paperback, and Audio

Excerpt from "Minds of Men:"

"Look sharp, everyone," Carl said after a while. Evelyn couldn't have said whether they'd been droning for minutes or hours in the cold, dense white of the cloud cover. "We should be overhead the French coast in about thirty seconds."

The men all reacted to this announcement with varying degrees of excitement and terror. Sean got up from his seat and came back to her, holding an awkward looking arrangement of fabric and straps.

Put this on, he thought to her. *It's your flak jacket. And your parachute is just there,* he said, pointing. *If the captain gives the order to bail out, you go, clip this piece into your 'chute, and jump out the biggest hole you can find. Do you understand? You do, don't you. This psychic thing certainly makes explaining things easier,* he finished with a grin.

Evelyn gave him what she hoped was a brave smile and took the flak jacket from him. It was deceptively heavy, and she struggled a bit with getting it on. Sean gave her a smile and a thumbs up, and then headed back to his station.

The other men were checking in and charging their weapons. A short time later, Evelyn saw through Rico's eyes as the tail gunner watched their fighter escort waggle their wings at the formation and depart. They didn't have the long-range fuel capability to continue all the way to the target.

Someday, that long-range fighter escort we were promised will materialize, Carl thought. His mind felt determinedly positive, like he was trying to be strong for the crew and not let them see his fear. That, of course, was an impossibility, but the crew took it well. After all, they were afraid, too. Especially as the formation had begun its descent to the attack altitude of 20,000 feet. Evelyn became gradually aware of

131

the way the men's collective tension ratcheted up with every hundred feet of descent. They were entering enemy fighter territory.

Yeah, and someday Veronica Lake will...ah. Never mind. Sorry, Evie. That was Les. Evelyn could feel the waist gunner's not-quite-repentant grin. She had to suppress a grin of her own, but Les' irreverence was the perfect tension breaker.

Boys will be boys, she sent, projecting a sense of tolerance. *But real men keep their private lives private.* She added this last with a bit of smug superiority and felt the rest of the crew's appreciative flare of humor at her jab. Even Les laughed, shaking his head. A warmth that had nothing to do with her electric suit enfolded Evelyn, and she started to feel like, maybe, she just might become part of the crew yet.

Fighters! Twelve o'clock high!

The call came from Alice. If she craned her neck to look around Sean's body, Evelyn could just see the terrifying rain of tracer fire coming from the dark, diving silhouette of an enemy fighter. She let the call echo down her own channels and felt her men respond, turning their own weapons to cover *Teacher's Pet's* flanks. Adrenaline surges spiked through all of them, causing Evelyn's heart to race in turn. She took a deep breath and reached out to tie her crew in closer to the Forts around them.

She looked through Sean's eyes as he fired from the top turret, tracking his line of bullets just in front of the attacking aircraft. His mind was oddly calm and terribly focused...as, indeed, they all were. Even young Lieutenant Bob was zeroed in on his task of keeping a tight position and making it that much harder to penetrate the deadly crossing fire of the Flying Fortress.

Fighters! Three o'clock low!

That was Logan in the ball turret. Evelyn felt him as he spun his turret around and began to fire the twin Browning AN/M2 .50 caliber machine guns at the sinister dark shapes rising up to meet them with fire.

Got 'em, Bobby Fritsche replied, from his position in the right waist. He, too, opened up with his own .50 caliber machine gun, tracking the barrel forward of the nose of the fighter formation, in order to "lead" their flight and not shoot behind them.

Evelyn blinked, then hastily relayed the call to the other girls in the formation net. She felt their acknowledgement, though it was almost an absentminded thing as each of the girls were focusing mostly on the communication between the men in their individual crews.

Got you, you Kraut sonofabitch! Logan exulted. Evelyn looked through his eyes and couldn't help but feel a twist of pity for the pilot of the German fighter as he spiraled toward the ground, one wing completely gone. She carefully kept that emotion from Logan, however, as he was concentrating on trying to take out the other three fighters who'd been in the initial attacking wedge. One fell victim to Bobby's relentless fire as he threw out a curtain of lead that couldn't be avoided.

Two back to you, tail, Bobby said, his mind carrying an even calm, devoid of Logan's adrenaline-fueled exultation.

Yup, Rico Martinez answered as he visually acquired the two remaining targets and opened fire. He was aided by fire from the aircraft flying off their right wing, the *Nagging Natasha.* She fired from her left waist and tail, and the two remaining fighters faltered and tumbled through the resulting crossfire. Evelyn watched through Rico's eyes as the ugly black smoke trailed the wreckage down.

Fighters! Twelve high!

Fighters! Two high!

The calls were simultaneous, coming from Sean in his top turret and Les on the left side. Evelyn took a deep breath and did her best to split her attention between the two of them, keeping the net strong and open. Sean and Les opened fire, their respective weapons adding a cacophony of pops to the ever-present thrum of the engines.

Flak! That was Carl, up front. Evelyn felt him take hold of the controls, helping the lieutenant to maintain his position in the formation as the Nazi anti-aircraft guns began to send up 20mm shells that blossomed into dark clouds that pocked the sky. One exploded right in front of *Pretty Cass'* nose. Evelyn felt the bottom drop out of her stomach as the aircraft heaved first up and then down. She held on grimly and passed on the wordless knowledge the pilots had no choice but to fly through the debris and shrapnel that resulted.

In the meantime, the gunners continued their rapid fire response to the enemy fighters' attempt to break up the formation. Evelyn took that knowledge—that the Luftwaffe was trying to isolate one of the Forts, make her vulnerable—and passed it along the looser formation net.

Shit! They got Liberty Belle*!* Logan called out then, from his view in the ball turret. Evelyn looked through his angry eyes, feeling his sudden spike of despair as they watched the crippled Fort fall back, two of her four engines smoking. Instantly, the enemy fighters swarmed like so many insects, and Evelyn watched as the aircraft yawed over and began to spin down and out of control.

A few agonizing heartbeats later, first one, then three more parachutes fluttered open far below. Evelyn felt Logan's bitter knowledge that there had been six other men on board that aircraft. *Liberty Belle* was one of the few birds flying without a psychic on board, and Evelyn suppressed a small, wicked feeling of relief that she hadn't just lost one of her friends.

Fighters! Twelve o'clock level!

* * * * *

Get "Minds of Men" now at:
https://www.amazon.com/dp/B0778SPKQV

Find out more about Kacey Ezell and "Minds of Men" at:
https://chriskennedypublishing.com

* * * * *

The following is an
Excerpt from Book One of the Revelations Cycle:

Cartwright's Cavaliers

Mark Wandrey

Available Now from Seventh Seal Press

eBook, Paperback, and Audio Book

Excerpt from "Cartwright's Cavaliers:"

The last two operational tanks were trapped on their chosen path. Faced with destroyed vehicles front and back, they cut sideways to the edge of the dry river bed they'd been moving along and found several large boulders to maneuver around that allowed them to present a hull-down defensive position. Their troopers rallied on that position. It was starting to look like they'd dig in when Phoenix 1 screamed over and strafed them with dual streams of railgun rounds. A split second later, Phoenix 2 followed on a parallel path. Jim was just cheering the air attack when he saw it. The sixth damned tank, and it was a heavy.

"I got that last tank," Jim said over the command net.

"Observe and stand by," Murdock said.

"We'll have these in hand shortly," Buddha agreed, his transmission interspersed with the thudding of his CASPer firing its magnet accelerator. "We can be there in a few minutes."

Jim examined his battlespace. The tank was massive. It had to be one of the fusion-powered beasts he'd read about. Which meant shields and energy weapons. It was heading down the same gap the APC had taken, so it was heading toward Second Squad, and fast.

"Shit," he said.

"Jim," Hargrave said, "we're in position. What are you doing?"

"Leading," Jim said as he jumped out from the rock wall.

* * * * *

Get "Cartwright's Cavaliers" now at:
https://www.amazon.com/dp/B01MRZKM95

Find out more about Mark Wandrey and the Four Horsemen Universe at:

https://chriskennedypublishing.com/the-four-horsemen-books/

* * * * *

The following is an
Excerpt from Book One of the Salvage Title Trilogy:

Salvage Title

Kevin Steverson

Available Now from Theogony Books

eBook, Paperback, and Audio Book

Excerpt from "Salvage Title:"

The first thing Clip did was get power to the door and the access panel. Two of his power cells did the trick once he had them wired to the container. He then pulled out his slate and connected it. It lit up, and his fingers flew across it. It took him a few minutes to establish a link, then he programmed it to search for the combination to the access panel.

"Is it from a human ship?" Harmon asked, curious.

"I don't think so, but it doesn't matter; ones and zeros are still ones and zeros when it comes to computers. It's universal. I mean, there are some things you have to know to get other races' computers to run right, but it's not that hard," Clip said.

Harmon shook his head. *Riiigghht,* he thought. He knew better. Clip's intelligence test results were completely off the charts. Clip opted to go to work at Rinto's right after secondary school because there was nothing for him to learn at the colleges and universities on either Tretra or Joth. He could have received academic scholarships for advanced degrees on a number of nearby systems. He could have even gone all the way to Earth and attended the University of Georgia if he wanted. The problem was getting there. The schools would have provided free tuition if he could just have paid to get there.

Secondary school had been rough on Clip. He was a small guy that made excellent grades without trying. It would have been worse if Harmon hadn't let everyone know that Clip was his brother. They lived in the same foster center, so it was mostly true. The first day of school, Harmon had laid down the law—if you messed with Clip, you messed up.

At the age of fourteen, he beat three seniors senseless for attempting to put Clip in a trash container. One of them was a Yalteen, a member of a race of large humanoids from two systems over. It wasn't a fair fight—they should have brought more people with them. Harmon hated bullies.

143

After the suspension ended, the school's Warball coach came to see him. He started that season as a freshman and worked on using it to earn a scholarship to the academy. By the time he graduated, he was six feet two inches with two hundred and twenty pounds of muscle. He got the scholarship and a shot at going into space. It was the longest time he'd ever spent away from his foster brother, but he couldn't turn it down.

Clip stayed on Joth and went to work for Rinto. He figured it was a job that would get him access to all kinds of technical stuff, servos, motors, and maybe even some alien computers. The first week he was there, he tweaked the equipment and increased the plant's recycled steel production by 12 percent. Rinto was eternally grateful, as it put him solidly into the profit column instead of toeing the line between profit and loss. When Harmon came back to the planet after the academy, Rinto hired him on the spot on Clip's recommendation. After he saw Harmon operate the grappler and got to know him, he was glad he did.

A steady beeping brought Harmon back to the present. Clip's program had succeeded in unlocking the container. "Right on!" Clip exclaimed. He was always using expressions hundreds or more years out of style. "Let's see what we have; I hope this one isn't empty, too." Last month they'd come across a smaller vault, but it had been empty.

Harmon stepped up and wedged his hands into the small opening the door had made when it disengaged the locks. There wasn't enough power in the small cells Clip used to open it any further. He put his weight into it, and the door opened enough for them to get inside. Before they went in, Harmon placed a piece of pipe in the doorway so it couldn't close and lock on them, baking them alive before anyone realized they were missing.

Daylight shone in through the doorway, and they both froze in place; the weapons vault was full.

* * * * *

Get "Salvage Title" now at:
https://www.amazon.com/dp/B07H8Q3HBV.

Find out more about Kevin Steverson and "Salvage Title" at:
http://chriskennedypublishing.com/.

* * * * *

Made in the USA
Coppell, TX
13 March 2021

51637554R00085